LINES CROSSED

CIN MEDLEY

LINES
Crossed
CIN MEDLEY

The characters in this book are not real people. They have been made up. They are by no means related to or pertain to anyone. This material is copyrighted. No portion of this book can be used without written permission from the publisher.

Published by Med's Pub Publishing
Copyright © 2019 Cin Medley
All Rights Reserved
ISBN-13: 978-0-9989748-6-6
Cover Design by: Amanda Walker P.A. and Design Services
Edited by: Kendra's Editing and Book Services- Kendra Gaither
Formatting by: Med's Pub Publishing

I want thank Melissa Schwab for taking the lead as my Alpha reader. Your words of encouragement and suggestions helped form this story. I thank you.

To my readers:

In the beginning stages of my writing career, I invented a security company called Blackshaw Security. The owner is a man named Joe Blackshaw. Along with his brother Al, they have been part of the last several books that I have written.

Many of you who know me have mentioned a few times that I should give Joe a story. Well, I decided to not only give Joe his story but to finally write a story for my sweet friend Veronica, who is the reason I write the naughty.

Al has since left my imaginary book world when he crossed the line and fell in love with Becca Storm from Within the Ashes. He did, however, come back for a brief moment in Secrets, to participate in the final showdown from Beautiful Liar, bringing with him Victoria Parker and Paul Simon.

I hope you enjoy this story because, when Lines are Crossed, sometimes beautiful things happen.

So, for my dear sweet friend Veronica, this is for you. I hope I make you proud.

PROLOGUE

"Listen, man, I need to head out. I miss my wife."

Joe laughed. "You've been gone for three days."

Al smiled at his brother. "That's three days too long. Listen, man, I hope one day you find what I have. A woman who will only see you. I never imagined feeling this way about someone, never thought I'd find what I have now. It's here." He tapped his chest. "It's so deep in here that I don't know how the hell I survived life without her."

Joe hugged his brother. "Not sure it's out there for me, but I will say this. I'm ready to take a fucking vacation. I even considered giving the business to Jason and getting out. Looking back on the life we've had, with our sister gone and Mom wanting some grandchildren, I think it's time I stopped near missing the bullet. After all this shit, I don't like feeling that I'm touchable now. This fucking shit is as real as it gets."

"No shit. That's what freaked Bec out. I didn't tell her much, but she doesn't want me anywhere near a gun. I don't blame her really, not after the shit she lived through. So, I support you. Hell, you're pushing forty-five; if anyone deserves a bit of happiness, it's you, big brother. Go, travel, do whatever feels good. Find a woman and settle down." Joe nodded his agreement as they made their way out of the hotel, and Al asked him, "I'm going to see Mom. You want to come with?"

"No, I think, after all this shit, I need a drink."

Al laughed. "You don't drink."

"I don't drink on the job or when we have a job. No more jobs, man, not for a while. I've got some thinking to do."

"Well, in a bottle is not the place to do it."

Joe laughed. "Go. See Mom. Tell her I'll come by before I head back to L.A. Tell Becca I send my love. You take care, brother."

They hugged, and Al got in the truck. Taking one last look at his brother, he nodded and drove away.

Joe stood on the street watching his brother disappear into traffic before he headed back inside to have himself a drink. There were so many things he needed to think about. But fuck if he wanted to. He more or less just felt like getting drunk. Walking into the bar of the hotel he'd been staying at, he sat on a stool and ordered a whiskey. Looking at the bartender, who smiled as she set his drink in front of him, he thought she was quite beautiful. As he put the glass to his mouth, his phone vibrated in his pocket. Pulling it out he looked at the caller ID. It wasn't a number he knew. Looking at the glass then at his phone, he hesitated. Choosing the phone, he answered it.

"Joe Blackshaw."

"Mr. Blackshaw, this is Emma Wilson. Victoria gave me your phone number. She said you have the number and address of the lawyer who holds the trust to my inheritance."

"I do. It's upstairs. Let me go up and get it. Give me a minute." He stood, dropping a twenty on the bar. A few minutes later, he was rattling off the number.

"Thank you."

"Emma, are you going to be all right?"

"I am. I'm taking my life back. Thank you again."

Joe went to say something, but she hung up. As he looked around the room, he knew he needed to go home. He didn't really need to get drunk. After packing his bag, he went to see his mother before he headed back to L.A. It was time he made a decision. Although, he already knew in his heart what he was going to do. He was done. Too many years had passed him by.

On the drive out to his mother's, his phone rang again. "Joe Blackshaw."

"Hi, Joe, it's Victoria."

"Everything all right?"

"Yeah, it's fine. I was wondering if you could help Emma. She is going to take her life back, and with less than a high school education, I was wondering if you could see her through all of this?"

He chuckled. "Yeah, not a problem. After this, I'm out. I'm resigning. I think I'm going to find me a good woman and settle down. Seems to be the thing to do."

She laughed. "Good luck, but you know we are hard to find."

"Yeah, I suppose you are. Just tell her to call me."

"Thanks, Joe, and good luck."

Pulling up to his mother's house, he felt a sense of calm wash over him. He always felt this way when he came here. Not sure why, but maybe it was the security he felt when he was a child. This was the home where he and his brothers and his sister grew up, and as he took in the view, he knew he was ready to retire. He just didn't want to do the risky job anymore. He was going back to L.A. to give the business to Jason. He had enough money to retire and live a good life.

He spent a few hours with his mom, and when Emma Wilson called again, he stayed until she got to town. After saying goodbye to his mother and promising to come back soon, he went to meet Emma at the lawyer's office.

All in all, it took a little over an hour to get her life back. He wished her well and headed to the airport, calling his brother Jason on the way.

"Hey, buddy, I hate to spring it on you like this, but I'm out. I'm giving it all to you."

"What the fuck are you talking about?"

Joe laughed. "The business. This last case made me realize I'm done. I was coming back, but I think I'm going to head up to the cabin for a while. I've got to clear my head. It's all yours. Take it."

"What if I don't want it?"

"You want it. You're just like we were, hungry for it. So, take the gift, little brother. I'm out."

"You're serious?"

"I am. Listen, I'll be back in a few weeks. I just need to calm the fuck down and take a look at my life. I'm forty-five. I've been doing this shit for twenty years now. I just need time to myself. We'll talk when I get back."

"Love you, man."

"Love you, too."

Joe headed to Minnesota. The company had a cabin up there, which they'd used on more than one occasion to hide a client or two. It was a good six and a half hours away, but he had nothing but time now. He smiled to himself. It was time for him to decompress.

CHAPTER ONE

Waking up to the sounds of nature always filled Joe with a sense of peace. The sounds of the little creek rolling over the rocks a few hundred yards from the cabin, which isn't really a cabin. Yes, it's made of logs, but it's not small.

Joe lay naked on his back looking at the ceiling. His life had been full. Three tours in Afghanistan, the death of their sister ending their lives. No one saw it coming. Life changed for him, his brothers, his mother. For a long time, none of them lived. They floated in their grief.

Joe had no idea how long he'd slept. To be honest, he didn't really care. Rolling out of bed, he grabbed a change of clothes from his bag and jumped in the shower, letting the hot water wash away the stress of the last several jobs. He threw on a pair of jeans and wandered over to the kitchen area to make some coffee. Walking out onto the back deck, he stood there listening to the silence. It was so quiet his ears were ringing. Birds chirped, and the water from the small creek rolled over the rocks, but it was still so quiet compared to the noise of L.A. or any other city he'd found himself in over the years. He wasn't sure he'd ever heard such quiet before.

His dreams, or nightmares really, stopped a few years ago, but he had learned to go on very little sleep. Twenty-five years of no sleep is more than enough. He served his country, did his time. He saved countless people had been shot a few times and had scars on his lower abdomen from being stabbed. His hand moved to the scars on his chest and arm, then to the healed stab wounds. More than once, he danced with the devil. It was this last case that had him rethinking his path in life.

He believed that his brother Al had the right idea of leaving this life for love. But Joe wasn't sure it was the life for him. He had only ever met one woman who sparked anything inside of him, any emotion, and when she found out what he did for a living, she walked away. He smiled, remembering how sweet she tasted. She took his heart with her when she left. He never allowed himself to care enough to try for something more. He had convinced himself he was better off. But that was fifteen years ago. Since then, he'd locked up his heart and his emotions, taking what was offered to him and moving on.

That life no longer appealed to Joe. He was done with condoms and random fucks. Fifteen years is a long time; that's how long it had been since the last time he felt the slow burn of making love to a woman. Standing on the deck, he could feel his cock getting harder. He wasn't the type of man to jack off; he preferred to fuck. Hard and to the point, it had only ever been for the satisfaction of the release. His life was too complicated for anything else, and it only happened once in a great while. Joe didn't go looking for sex, for his next conquest, but when the opportunity presented itself, he took it. They were women he'd meet in a bar, after a case, while he was there with his brothers toasting to their success.

Joe wasn't a drinking man; one or two glasses of whiskey and he was always the first to leave and the last to show up. Women usually followed him out the door. Looking down at himself, he looked at the scars marring his body, which was nothing but muscle. Six feet and three inches of nothing but solid muscle. If he were a woman, he would be terrified of him. He chuckled at the thought. All of his brothers were tall, and all of them had huge cocks. Not that he went looking, but they were all about a year apart in age, so they spent a lot of time together.

Looking through the trees and down to the trail leading up from where he'd parked, he felt like a run. Dumping his coffee, he went back and changed into his running gear and took off through the woods. Pounding the unlevel terrain brought back memories he thought he'd laid to rest. Memories of their time at war, the desert heat, the adrenaline rush of fear every time they needed to drive somewhere. Too many of his buddies died along the roads by roadside bombs.

His mind wandered. Would he have stayed in if his sister hadn't been murdered? She was such a spectacular human being. So gentle and kind, the complete opposite of the boys. She was his baby sister, the youngest of the six of them, and was fiercely protected as she grew up. Joe could remember how happy she was on her wedding day. But that fucker hurt her, hurt her to the point of killing her. She didn't tell anyone. They thought it was because she truly loved him. The fucker was in prison now, and Joe, along with his brothers, knew his body would never be found once he got out. He was a dead man walking.

Shaking his head to get the memories out, he looped around and headed back to the cabin. Once there, he showered. After pulling on a pair of jeans, he made himself some breakfast. He was having a hard time not working. It's what he did. How was he supposed to do this? To just stop? He went and sat on the deck, barefoot, shirtless, his jeans half-buttoned. This is the life he wanted. Who gave a shit if he looked like this? No one, and it felt good to just be. If he could only get his mind to shut off.

Closing his eyes, he was enjoying the warmth of the sun filtering through the trees on his face. A few moments later, he heard what sounded like a branch cracking. His body instantly switched into a hyper-aware mode. He was on his feet, his head listening to the shuffling of the earth as it moved under the pressure of whatever was coming toward him. Then it stopped. He moved inside the door, grabbing his gun off the counter. It was the scream that had him moving off the deck barefoot, across the lawn. Again, the scream came, and he was moving right towards it. He stopped in his tracks when he saw a woman kneeling on the ground. His eyes darted around, looking to see if someone else was there.

"Are you all right?" His voice was barely a whisper.

The woman jumped to her feet and moved away from him. To Joe, she looked freaked out. She just stood there with tears running down her face, eyeing him up and down. Her eyes landed on the gun in his hand. "What the fuck?" Her voice was barely audible.

Joe's eyes shifted from hers, searching around. "Are you all right?" His eyes locked with hers.

He watched her swallow hard. "I'm fine."

"Then what the hell are you screaming like that for?" he snapped at her.

She raised her eyebrows at him. "I'm in the middle of the woods. I felt like I needed to scream. I think you might be wound a bit tight."

He shook his head. "Stop screaming like that on my land. If you're going to scream, go home and do it."

"Your land? I'm sorry, you must be mistaken."

"No, sweetheart, my house is right there. My land." He smiled at her, pushing his gun in the back of his pants. He saw her eyes follow his arm as it moved. He also saw her lick her lips when they landed on his stomach. "You have a good day." He turned with a huge smile on his face and headed back to his cabin.

Going up the steps and into the cabin, he set his gun on the counter and grabbed a t-shirt. His smile never wavered. He had no idea who she was. She looked like she had been running. Turning to look at the door, thinking maybe he could get laid, he nodded his head. But he was here to decompress, not get laid. Chuckling, he made some lunch and put her out of his mind. This was about coming to terms with facts. He was too old to keep doing this shit. He wasn't a lifer, or was he?

Taking his lunch, he went into the dining room and sat at the table to eat. Then he grabbed a book and headed out to the deck to read. It was the only way to stop his mind from convincing him this was the stupidest idea he'd ever had.

The words on the page didn't even resonate in his brain. They were just black letters on the white pages. Snapping the book shut, he set it on the table next to him and looked out at the world. His mind would not shut off, and he really needed a distraction. Looking around, he tried to remember what things he enjoyed in life. Not much. He liked shooting. He loved solving complicated puzzles, but he had a whole team to help him.

Here he was, in one of the most beautiful places he had ever seen, so quiet, so void of traffic, and the only thing he could think about was working the next case. "Man, I am so fucked." It really was time for him to just decompress. Only, he couldn't figure out how the hell to do it.

His eyes closed. "Sleep." He needed to sleep. It was easier than he thought to fall into a good slumber in the middle of the day. But when he heard a twig snap, his eyes popped open, darting around with the precision of a cat on the hunt. Another snap of a twig, the rustle of the leaves. His hearing sharp as a tack, he moved his head and saw her before she saw him. The woman from the woods. She was walking up to him. He didn't move.

"I just wanted to apologize for being so rude to you earlier. I was on your land."

Joe chuckled. "I know. What can I do for you?" He didn't mean to sound rude, but he was pretty sure, looking at her, that she was a pampered princess. Not the type of woman he would want to spend time with. They were such snobs. He preferred a woman who wasn't afraid to get her hands dirty. A woman who wouldn't make a federal case out of a broken fingernail. His eyes moved to her hands, which were perfectly manicured.

"Well," she began. He raised his eyes to look at her face. Makeup perfectly applied. "I figured I would come and introduce myself, seeing as how we are neighbors. My name is Roni. I'm up here," she turned to look at their surroundings, "to decompress."

Joe sat there looking at her. She had a nice ass—full, round in her tight jeans. He smiled, shaking his head. He knew why she was there, but was he willing to fuck her? As he raised his eyebrows at the thought, she turned and smiled at him.

"See something you like?"

Joe laughed, getting out of the chair. "Sweetheart, I don't know what you are up to, but I'm not buying the act. Your demeanor, your outfit, the fact that you are standing on my porch dressed the way you are, says that you want one thing from me."

He watched the fury build in her eyes as he spoke. "So, what, when a guy comes on to a woman, it's acceptable, but when a woman expresses her interest in a man, she's labeled? If you were to walk up to me in a bar, I would be expected to be flattered?"

"Well, there's your problem." He moved to walk away. "I wouldn't be the man who walked up to you. Trust me when I tell you this. You aren't my type." He walked off the deck, headed to the creek. His smile didn't leave his lips. Oh, he wanted to fuck her all right, but on his terms, not hers. He wasn't going to get involved with the game she was obviously playing with him.

He stood by the creek waiting to hear her leave. Instead, he heard her footsteps crunching on leaves as she walked up next to him. "So, what's your type? I suppose the model-thin type? No ass, no boobs, no brain?"

Looking out into the woods, he chuckled. "Not a woman who is afraid to get dirty, and," he paused, "certainly not a woman who walks through the woods in high heels." His eyes shifted to her feet. "Now, if you'll excuse me." He turned and headed back to the house with a huge smile on his face.

He wasn't sure if she stayed down by the creek or if she left. He didn't really care. Well, he cared because he really wanted to get laid, but sex wasn't going to help him come to terms with what his life had become. The choice he was making. Putting his head back, his eyes closed he moaned. "Fuck."

"It's the reason I came over here. I know I could use a release of tension." The voice came from the back door.

Joe laughed, standing and moving to the kitchen. "Listen, sweetheart—"

"Roni, my name is Roni. I'm nobody's sweetheart."

"I'm not going to fuck you," he stated.

"Oh, trust me, I get that. Fine. Your loss," she snapped. Turning, she walked off the deck and disappeared into the woods.

Joe shut the door, picked up his gun, and headed to the bedroom. He needed to sleep. Lying on his back looking at the ceiling, his cock semi-hard, he had to admit, she had a mighty fine ass. An ass he could most assuredly get lost in. It had been months since he sunk himself into a woman who was more than skin and bones. Joe found that he preferred women with substance to their bodies. He hated when bones protruded through the soft flesh. Joe draped his arm across his eyes. It wasn't what he wanted. He wanted a life, and a woman he could spend that life with. Getting laid was easy. Roni proved that to him.

Just thinking about that ass was making him hard. He wasn't going to get any sleep at this rate. He didn't want to fucking jack off, but his cock was starting to ache. He got up and found himself standing on the deck, wondering which direction she went. He figured, since she was willing and he needed a release, why not? And, yes, he was bastard enough that he would use her.

Stepping off the deck, he headed in the direction he'd gone when he heard her scream. He made it to the edge of the lawn when he looked up and she was standing on the path looking at him. His eyes traveled down her body to her feet, and he saw she had changed her shoes. His smile was slow as he moved up her body. Her jeans were tight, but she had changed her shirt. Her breasts were definitely more than a handful and had his gaze pausing at her chest. As he looked up past her neck, she drew her un-glossed lip between her teeth. With her face void of makeup, her eyes shone a piercing green. They stood there looking at each other. Joe felt his cock hardening in his jeans.

He was a bit confused by her appearance. "What do you want from me?" His voice was deep, his words sharp.

Her tongue slowly slid across her lips. "I just... I just, I don't know."

Neither of them moved. He needed to get control of his growing lust. His quick growing desire to fuck this woman into next week was getting the best of him. Joe was not a man who lost control. Then again, he'd never been in this situation, where no one was depending on him. He was free from any bonds or obligations and standing in front of him was the perfect woman, with a deliciously curvy body and the sweetest plump lips he wanted to devour.

"Why are you here?"

"My family owns a house up here. I needed to escape my life for a while."

"Does that life include a husband?" He didn't want any part of something like that.

"No, not married."

"Engaged?"

"Not anymore."

His eyes locked on hers. He knew there was something more; he just wasn't sure he wanted to get that involved. "I don't want anything more than this."

She nodded her head. "Neither do I. My life—"

Joe cut her off, "Don't. I don't want to know anything about you." He stepped forward, his hand reaching forward. He wrapped his hand in her hair, pulling it tight against her head. "I might get rough. It's been a while." His mouth was nearly on top of hers.

She swallowed roughly. "I don't want it sweet. I want to feel. I want to be sore when we are done. I want to know in the morning that I've been thoroughly fucked." Her voice cracked a few times as she spoke.

Joe smiled. "Oh, trust me, sweetheart. It will be days before you forget I was inside of you."

"Then what are you waiting for?" she whispered.

Joe slammed his mouth down on hers, forcing his tongue between her lips. She met his advance with just as much desire, biting his lip as he pulled back in shock. She tasted so sweet. He was fully hard now, his cock pushing on his jeans. When he picked her up, she wrapped her legs around him, and he carried her back to the house, kicking the door shut behind them. Dropping her on the bed, he stepped back to look at her.

"Take your shirt off." He peeled his own t-shirt off then turned his eyes back to her body. When he looked at her, his breath hitched. She had bruises on her ribs. "What the fuck?"

"I fell down the stairs. It's nothing." Her eyes never left his.

Joe knew better. He had seen women after they'd been beaten. Slowly, he moved his eyes up her body, looking at her chest, and a moan slipped from his throat. Her breasts were fucking huge, perfect. Nipples hard and huge. The way they relaxed across her body, he knew they were real. His cock twitched in his jeans. Leaning in, he unzipped her jeans, pulling them off. "Fuck." She was shaved clean.

His hands unclasped his own jeans, dropping them to the floor and releasing his cock. Her eyes moved down his body. He heard her moan. Leaning over, he opened the drawer and pulled out a packet of condoms. Ripping one off and dropping the rest on the bed, he smiled when her eyes got big.

Joe opened one and rolled it on. His hands on her hips, he flipped her over. "On your knees." He moaned at his first look at her plump ass. He wanted to touch it, devour it.

Roni smiled at him, pulling up on her knees. Joe nearly came right there looking at her. "Damn."

His hands reached out, wrapping around her hips to pull her toward him. He ran his thumb through her folds, making sure she was ready, then up the crack of her ass before slowly pushing inside of her. The slow burn nearly unhinged him. His eyes watched his cock as he pushed deep, and her lush body swallowed him. "Fuck, you're tight," he ground out.

He moved a few times to let her get used to his size, and then he let go, slamming deep into her. She met him thrust for thrust. Joe was almost embarrassed at how fast he came. Watching her ass as he slammed into her made him lose his mind. But he didn't care. He needed the release. When he finished, he pulled out of her and headed to the bathroom to dispose of the condom, leaving her with her ass in the air on the edge of the bed.

When he turned back to the bedroom, she was lying on her stomach on the bed. Standing in the doorway admiring her fucking kick ass body, he grew hard again. He walked out as she rolled over, a small smile on her face when she saw he was semi-hard. Joe grabbed another condom off the packet and climbed on the bed, taking one of her nipples in his mouth. When she arched her back, he slid his hand under her, lifting her up. She ended up sitting on his thighs while they kissed one another.

She wrapped her hand around his cock, drawing a moan from deep within while she worked him into a full-blown erection. Taking the condom out of his hand, she tore it open and rolled it on. Joe grabbed her thighs and lifted her onto his cock.

"Oh, God," she moaned as he filled her.

Wrapping his hands under her arms, holding her in place so he could kiss her, he pulled her to his chest. Her hips gently rocked against him.

Pushing up, he laid her back, taking what he wanted from her, watching her perfect tits bounce with each thrust. Her body felt soft and full against his. He was in some sort of euphoric trance of sexual desire. They fucked for a long time, kissing every now and then. Joe pinched her nipples when he wasn't biting them. He locked her knee in the crook of his arm, opening her wider, and slammed into her until he released.

Exhausted, he pulled out and flopped onto the bed next to her. She rolled over with her back to him. He lay there looking at her. She was glorious, and she felt amazing. But he couldn't figure out why he felt like shit for doing what he just did.

Finally deciding he didn't want to care because she knew his expectations, he pulled off the condom, tying a knot, and dropped it on the floor. His eyes moved to her back again. Taking a deep breath, he opened his mouth to say something when she swung her legs over the side of the bed. He watched in silence as she got dressed. Then, without a glance backward, she walked out the door.

CHAPTER TWO

Roni couldn't believe she'd just given herself to a complete stranger. Her legs wouldn't carry her fast enough out the door. She had to stop herself from throwing up. It was pitch black out as she ran through the woods. Not knowing where she was going, she just ran as the tears fell down her face. Stopping to catch her breath, she let it go. The scream came from deep in her chest.

What had she done? She had sex with a man she met in the woods, a man made of nothing but pure sin. He was fucking beautiful, but she knew it was the worst thing she could have done. Until three days ago, she'd been engaged to be married. Her mother was still planning the wedding.

No one knew she walked into her apartment to find her fiancé fucking some woman against the wall in their living room. No one knew she stood there and watched as the only man she ever loved came inside of that woman, unprotected. No one knew she stood there and watched him kiss her with such passion like he had *never* kissed her. No one knew she stood there and listened to him whisper to her that he loved her. No one knew she took off her ring, set it on the table, and walked out. No one knew until the door slammed behind her.

She'd got in her car and rushed to the airport, flying here, to the only place she knew he wouldn't find her. Where she knew she was safe from his fists, from his kicks, from his hands that left marks and bruises all over her body. Where she knew she was safe from being raped by him, the only man she'd ever loved. Escaping him wouldn't be easy, especially since he was her father's choice. Her father's lawyer.

Sinking to the ground, she leaned against a tree and cried. She didn't hear the twigs breaking as he approached her. She didn't see him as he crouched down in front of her. When her tears dried up, she opened her eyes to see him, the beautiful stranger who just fucked her into next week. He picked her up and carried her back to his house. Sitting her on the porch swing, he went in and got her a glass of water. She took it from him, drinking the whole thing at once, then handed it back to him. He set it on the table as he pulled another chair forward to sit in front of her.

"What was that about in there?" His eyes never left hers.

"It was exactly what I wanted. Why does it matter?"

"It matters. Why were you out there crying, if it's what you wanted?"

"You made it perfectly clear that it was what it was, so why do you care?"

She watched anger grow in his eyes. "I'm not accustomed to a woman running out of my bedroom when I'm done."

"What, did you expect me to stay and snuggle, cuddle with you? Because I'm almost positive you aren't that kind of man."

Joe sat there looking at her. "You didn't make a sound." His voice was softer this time.

"Isn't that what all men want in a woman they are just fucking? No sound? No complications? Just a body to fuck, a body to release with? Listen, I appreciate the gesture of gallantness you're displaying here, but it's being wasted. Thank you for that. I needed it." She needed to know she wasn't worth anything but a good fuck. "I need to go." She stood up, but his hands moved to rest on her hips. "Don't be kind.

Somehow, I don't think it's in your nature. It would be an insult to my intelligence."

He let her go, and she walked off his porch and made her way back to her family's house. She couldn't stay here now. She needed to go back and end her relationship. She needed to tell her parents what he does to her, why she can't marry him.

Washing her face, she grabbed a few things and headed back to the airport, hoping the plane was still there. Five hours later, she pulled up to her parents' house; well, if you want to call a fifteen-bedroom mansion a house, then that is what it is. Walking in the front door, she was greeted by the maid.

"Miss Holloway, your mother and father have been going crazy with worry. Mr. Eden filed a missing person report on you. My God, child, where have you been?"

"I'm fine, Alice. Where are my parents?"

"They are in the living room. Mr. Eden just left. Should I call him?"

"No, Alice, please don't call him. I need to speak to my parents, then I will call him."

"Very well, miss."

Roni walked into the living room to find her parents sitting and talking to a man in a suit. Her mother saw her and burst into fake tears, rushing toward her. She grabbed her, causing Roni to wince in pain. "Where have you been? Tony has been worried sick. We have been worried sick."

Roni hugged her mother. "I'm fine, Mom. I just needed some time to think. I'm not going to marry Tony."

"Nonsense. We will talk about this later." She watched her mother turn to the man in the suit. "I guess the mystery is solved. Thank you so much for coming."

Roni hated the way her mother dismissed people. She stood there like the dutiful daughter and watched her mother ignore her and usher the man out of the room.

Her father stood there looking at her. "What happened?"

"I can't marry him, Daddy. I won't marry him. I found him with another woman in our living room. He was fucking her against the wall. He told her he loved her. He doesn't want to marry me."

"He told us you had a fight because he had to go back to D.C.?"

"He's full of shit."

"Veronica, Tony Eden is the best thing to happen to you. He is a good man." Her father always sang his praises.

"Is he, Daddy? Is he really? Tell me, what do you know about him?" she snapped.

"Veronica!" her mother shouted. "Do not speak to your father in that manner. We didn't raise you to be a heathen."

Roni busted out laughing. "A heathen, Mother? Really?" She dropped her bag on the floor and pulled off her shirt. "Are these the praises you want to sing about your precious Tony Eden?"

Her parents stood there looking at the bruises on her midsection. "What is this?" her father demanded.

"This is what happens when I don't do what he says, or if I just get in his way. These are marks from his fists. I wasn't ready when he walked in the door a week ago. You know the night we all had dinner? Remember, Mother, you asked me what was wrong, why I wasn't talking. Tony told you I was tired. He told me if I opened my mouth that it would be ten times worse when we got home."

"Veronica, I don't believe you," her mother chastised.

"Of course, you don't. Why would you? I am not marrying him. I won't live like this anymore." She grabbed her shirt and her bag. Walking out of the room, she headed upstairs. Halfway up, the front door opened and in walked Tony.

"Oh my God, Roni, what the hell happened to you?" He rushed toward her.

"No!" she yelled. "Stay away from me. We are done."

He kept coming, grabbing her by the arm. "You fucking little bitch," he whispered in her ear. "I am going to show you what done means."

"Let me go!" she yelled.

"You're coming home with me." He pulled her arm, pushing her in front of him.

"No!" She jerked her arm out of his grip and fell down the stairs.

Her father had walked into the front hall after she yelled the first time. He saw the whole thing happen and rushed to her side, as Tony flew down the stairs. She lay on her back looking at the ceiling, tears running down the side of her face.

Her father gently ran his thumb over her cheek. "Veronica, sweetheart. Are you hurt?"

Her eyes shifted to his. "No, Daddy. Please make him leave. He's going to hurt me again. Please," she whispered.

Her father looked up at Tony. "I think you should leave. She'll be fine here."

"But, sir, I'm leaving in the morning for D.C. We are leaving in the morning."

"No, we are not. I'm staying here. You should leave."

Tony looked at her, his hand coming up to wipe her tears, but she flinched and moved her head away from him. "Don't fucking touch me. You will never touch me again."

"Aww, sweetheart. What happened to you? Why are you acting like this?" Tony looked at her father. "Sir, I think she might be having a mental breakdown. Maybe you should think about getting her some professional help."

Roni saw her father's eyes. "You need to leave now, Tony."

Tony stared at her father. "Yes, sir." Looking down at Roni, he seethed. "I'll see you when I get back on Friday."

She closed her eyes. "No, you won't. This is over. We are over. Please, just get out."

She started to sit up, her mother handing her shirt over. Roni heard the door close just as her mother said, "You should be ashamed of yourself, throwing yourself down the stairs like that. You will go home to him, and you will marry him. You are thirty years old. You've had enough time to flaunt yourself around. He will make you a respectable woman in society."

Roni put on her shirt. "You know what, Mother? He took my virginity. I have never flaunted myself anywhere. I am not going to marry him. Is that what you want for me, Mother? A man who beats me?"

"Did you ever wonder why he did it? Do you think that maybe your mouth got you slapped around? If you would just keep your mouth shut, maybe he wouldn't hit you. Maybe if you lost some weight, he would want to be with you."

"That's enough, Elizabeth! This is our daughter. I will not allow any man to hurt her. This marriage is off. I will not allow her to be beaten like this. I saw the whole thing. I heard what he said to her. Now, it's done."

Roni turned to her father, hugging him. "Thank you, Daddy."

"I'll be a laughing stock. How will I explain this to our friends?" Her mother sniffled.

"Tell them the truth. The great Tony Eden has a problem with his temper and likes to beat up women," Roni snapped. Turning, she looked at her father. "Daddy, can I stay here for a bit? I need to regroup."

"You always have a home here. Go on up to your room. I need to make some phone calls." He kissed her on the forehead.

Roni got up and made her way to her old room. Lying on the bed, she let it all go, crying herself to sleep.

Joe watched her walk away. There was something more going on with this woman. His inner investigator told him not to let her go. But there was nothing he could do short of kidnapping her.

Picking himself up, he went back into the cabin and shut everything off. He was fucking tired. Walking into the bedroom, he saw the packet of condoms laying on the bed. His mind moved to fifteen minutes ago when he sunk his cock deep inside that perfect woman. Who was she? He didn't have a clue, but damn if she wasn't the best feeling he had ever felt. Somehow, he didn't think she was the kind of woman who just fucked a man and left. Stripping off his clothes, he lay on the bed. He could still smell her perfume. When he closed his eyes, she was there, her beautiful ass perched up in the air. The feel of the burn as he pushed inside of her. "Fuck." He had never had residual thoughts of a woman like this. Finally, sleep won over. He needed to decompress. Releasing felt so fucking good.

His sleep was invaded by her, the beautiful woman covered in bruises. His eyes popped open. "Fuck, she was beaten." He sat up, looked around. It was light out. Pulling on his jeans and shirt, he grabbed his boots and headed out to find her. Something deep inside of him knew there was more going on than she was saying.

As he walked through the woods, he saw a house around the bend of the creek. That had to be her place. There was no answer when he knocked on the door, so he looked in through the windows, but he could see the place was empty. "Where are you?"

As he walked back, he pulled her face up in his memory. Those green eyes, they were haunting. Her name was Roni. She had green eyes, reddish blonde hair, a fucking ass that would stop traffic, and the most perfect tits a man could imagine. Shaking his head, Joe knew this woman was not a quick fuck he had. She wasn't even a one-night stand. She managed to sear herself into his brain.

He spent the next few days trying to get her out of his head. At least he wasn't freaking out about walking away from his life. A life he needed to get back to, a life he needed to end. He knew now he didn't want to do this anymore. He was sure now that he was walking away.

After a week had passed, the woman still in his mind, he grabbed his shit and headed out. When he hit the highway headed to Minneapolis, he called Jason.

"Hey, man."

"Jesus, Joe, where the hell have you been? Your phone is off."

"No shit, I told you I needed some time to decompress. What's going on?"

"Senator Holloway has been calling. He wants you to call him."

"Jason, I'm out. I'm not taking any more cases. Can you get the jet to Minneapolis? I'm heading back."

"It's sitting on the tarmac; I sent it when the senator called. I was coming to get you in a day or two. Call him back. He's called three times already, sounded desperate."

"Fuck," he muttered. "Yeah, I'll call him. See you in a few hours."

As he walked up the stairs of the plane, his phone rang. Pulling it out of his pocket he swiped it on. "Joe Blackshaw."

"Joe, Michael Holloway. How are you?"

Joe chuckled. "Well, I was doing good. I was on vacation. What can I do for you?" Joe knew what he wanted. He was finding it hard to tell him no.

"Listen, there is some shit going on with my daughter. I was wondering if I could hire you to keep an eye on her for a while? We've discovered some discrepancies in her relationship, and I'm a bit fearful for her safety."

"Mike, I've retired. I'm just on my way back to sign all the papers giving control of the business to Jason. I'm too old for this shit."

"Is he as good as you?"

"He's my little brother. He's good."

"You sure you wouldn't reconsider for me? I will make it worth your while."

Joe laughed. "Mike, I have more than enough money. I'm too old for this shit. I had a few wake-up calls these past few years, and I think I want more out of my life. No amount of money can lure me back in. Jason is a good man and can get the job done. I will, however, for you, oversee it. I'm not getting involved, but I will keep my eye on him. I'm only going to be around for a few weeks, long enough to pack up my life and sell my apartment, then I'm gone."

"Thanks, Joe. I'll call your brother and give him all the details. Talk soon."

"Take care, Mike."

Joe disconnected the call and sat back in his seat. "Fucking privileged asshole." He liked Mike; he did do a lot of great shit for the state, but no way did he want to fucking babysit his princess of a daughter.

Closing his eyes, he put his head back and waited to take off. Five hours later, he was pulling up in front of his office. When he walked in, the sweet little secretary stood. "Mr. Blackshaw, welcome back." She smiled at him. Joe knew she wanted him, but there was no way. She was one of those princesses, always perfect.

"Thanks, Sherry. Is Jason in his office?"

"Yes, he is. I have all your messages here." She put her hand out full of pink pieces of paper.

He laughed. "Not my messages anymore. Give them to Jason," he said as he walked past her and into Jason's office.

"Hey," Jason said as he got up to hug his brother.

Joe sat in a chair opposite the oversized desk. "So, I talked to Holloway. It's all yours. If you run into any trouble, give me a call. I'm going home to pack. I'm taking the cabin, think I'll stay up there for a while. It's going to take a lot to get my fucking head out of this shit."

"I don't know what's in your head. What the hell happened that brought all this on?"

Joe sat there looking at him. "I think I'm just burnt out. I'm forty-five years old. I think I want some kids, a wife, a fucking life. I'm ready to settle down. Spending those ten days up at the cabin was good. It took a great deal to get my head in some sort of order. I still have a great deal more shit rolling around in there. But I figured, as long as I have this life here, I'm not going to let it go. So, I'm here to pack up my life and sell my apartment. I'm out."

"Wait a minute. I want your fucking apartment. I'll buy it."

Joe laughed. "You got a million dollars?"

Jason busted out laughing. "No way is that place worth a million."

"Well, I'll have it appraised and give you first crack at it. But I'm heading home. You got everything covered here? I'll get in touch with the lawyers and have everything transferred over into your name."

"Yeah, we're going by Holloway's in the morning to get all the details. Do you want me to fill you in?"

"Nope, I want nothing to do with it. I told him I would be here for a while and, if you needed help, I would help. But, Jason," he stood up, moving to the door, "don't need me."

Joe moved into his office and grabbed his personal things then headed out. When he got home, he stripped and crashed. He found himself looking forward to retiring. To doing nothing, to not having to jet all over the country. To not having to stay up for days at a time. He was done.

CHAPTER THREE

Roni stayed in her room for a few days. Alice brought up her food. She slept most of the time, and when she wasn't sleeping, she was thinking of the stranger she'd let fuck her. He was right when he said she would feel him for days after. Every time she sat up, she felt him. She thought about him, the way he kissed her, the way he was slow at first and then fucked her hard. Who was he? Why did he come after her?

She shouldn't have been thinking about the beautiful stranger. Hell, she didn't even know his name. Her life was in shambles. She needed to get her clothes and her things from the apartment she shared with Tony. Finally, she got dressed and made her way downstairs. Her father was in the living room talking to two men. She smiled at him as she moved past the doorway.

"Veronica, honey, can you come in here? I want you to meet someone."

She walked into the room looking like shit. A smile crossed her lips when she thought about how she'd stripped herself bare for the beautiful stranger. He preferred her that way. One of the men stood. "This is Jason Blackshaw. I hired him to keep an eye on you. I don't trust Tony. Not after hearing what he said to you."

"Daddy, is this necessary? I don't think Tony is stupid enough to come at me again."

The guy, Jason, spoke. "Miss Holloway, I just want you to know that we have some experience with situations like yours. Our sister was murdered by her husband. He beat her to death. We didn't know he was hurting her. Like you, she kept it to herself. Men like Mr. Eden should be stopped. They need to be stopped. We will keep you safe. One of us will be with you at all times."

She smiled. "You say we. Who are we?"

"Well, me, this is my brother Ben, and we have about thirty more guys. But it will be either me or Ben who is with you at all times. The others will just blend into the background."

Roni laughed. "Jesus, Dad, you didn't need to hire a freaking army. Tony isn't stupid enough to hurt me again. You're a senator, and he likes his job."

"Well, that's going to be a problem because he doesn't have a job anymore."

"What? You fired him?" Roni was shocked.

Her father stood and moved toward her. "Veronica, you are my only daughter. If I had known he was hurting you, it would have never gotten this far. Why didn't you tell me?"

She felt the tears building. "Because I was afraid. He said he would kill me if I ruined his career. That he was only marrying me because of you."

Her father wrapped his arms around her. "Aww, sweetheart, there isn't anything on this planet that is worth you. Don't you know that? He always seemed like a good man. I just wanted a good life for you."

"I know, Daddy. I know. He'll be back soon, though, and I need to get my things from the apartment."

Jason interrupted, "We will go with you, and we'll take the police with us so there are no misunderstandings. Whenever you are ready. We aren't going anywhere."

She nodded, wiping her face. "I just want to grab something to eat, and then I'll change. Maybe fifteen minutes?"

"I'll be right here."

“Thank you.” She kissed her father on the cheek and left the room. Going to the kitchen, she ran into her mother.

“Well, it’s about time you got your lazy ass out of bed. Now, when are you going to make up with Tony? I spoke to him this morning, and he is very remorseful about what happened.”

Roni stood there looking at her mother. “He was fucking another woman in my living room. There is no coming back from that. Get over it, Mother, I’m not going back.” She moved past her and into the kitchen. She wasn’t hungry anymore, so she headed up the back staircase and changed her clothes.

When she hit the bottom of the stairs, the front door opened, and Tony walked in. Not knowing what to do, she screamed, just as he grabbed her by the arm, backhanding her and knocking her to the floor. “Fucking bitch, you got me fired. I told you what was going to happen.” No sooner did the words come out of his mouth, he was slammed against the door.

“Ben, call the police.” Jason looked at Tony, who was easily a head shorter than him, and leaned in. “That will be the last time you touch her. I’m here to tell you, if you get near her again, I won’t hesitate.”

“Who the fuck are you? Get your hands off me or I’ll sue your ass.”

Jason smiled then punched him in the stomach. “Give it your best shot, asshole. Touch her again and I won’t hesitate. Do you understand me?”

Tony opened his mouth, and Jason punched him again. “Do you understand me?”

Coughing, Tony sputtered out, “Yeah, fucker.”

Jason pulled him up and wrapped his wrists with a zip-tie. “You’re going to jail, asshole.” He shoved Tony against the door.

Roni’s father helped her up, just as her mother came in with some ice, shooting daggers at Tony.

His eyes never left Roni’s. “What, is he the reason you are leaving me?” He nodded to Jason.

Roni just shook her head and moved to the living room with her parents.

Jason stood there staring at him. "What the fuck are you looking at?" Tony asked.

"A fucking asshole just like you murdered my sister. I want to see what a real fucking asshole looks like. You barked up the wrong tree."

"You can't fucking touch me. I'll bury you in court, you fuck."

Jason laughed. "Go for it. Do your best, but you'll be wasting your time."

"I don't know who the hell you think you are, but you are going down."

Jason just laughed at him. They stood there staring at each other until the police came. Roni filed charges of assault and battery. Jason took her to the police station to sign all the papers, and then an officer accompanied her to their apartment. Jason called in his crew, and it took an hour to get everything she had out of the place. Roni placed her key on the counter and walked out.

Not saying a word all the way back to her parents' place, she sat looking out the window. When Jason pulled up, she opened the door and got out, going directly to her bedroom, and there she stayed. Her things were brought up and put away by the maid, with the exception of a few boxes and her jewelry.

Sitting in the middle of her bed, she realized that she was just as the mysterious man made of nothing but pure sin said she was. A princess, with fancy clothes, expensive jewelry, and a driver. She had never had to work for anything her whole life. She walked to the mirror in her room and stood there looking at herself. Everything about her was perfect, or was perceived to be perfect. She took off her t-shirt to look at her bruises. The one on her cheek could stand to use some makeup, but she didn't want to be that girl anymore. That girl only made men like Tony Eden think she was valuable. The man up at the cabin didn't think she was valuable. She was just sex, pure sex.

Not sure if that excited her or pissed her off, but it stirred something in her. Closing her eyes, she could still hear his voice when he pulled her jeans off. Tony always made her shave. He said he hated when pubic hair got in his mouth or on him, not that he did that to her. In fact, he never pleasured her. Neither did the mystery man. But he did touch her. He bit and sucked her nipples. Tony only ever grabbed them when he was coming, and rarely kissed her before, during, or after sex.

He was just like the mystery man; he finished then got up and walked out. But the mystery man came back for more. He held her for a few minutes, devoured her mouth, and then sent her to the moon and back. Never had she had an orgasm like that.

Turning sideways, Roni looked at her body. She wasn't thin, not like the woman Tony had against the wall. She could stand to lose some weight. Tony kept telling her she was fat, too fat for him to enjoy. She couldn't see her ribs, and when she sucked in her stomach, she couldn't see her hip bones. Maybe she should start to exercise, maybe go on a diet.

Her fingers moved up and unhooked her bra before dropping it on the floor. She smiled. She did have big boobs, bigger than she should. They were only this big because she was heavier than most of the women she knew. But the stranger thought they were nice. He'd spent a great deal of time touching them.

Shaking her head, she grabbed a sweatshirt. "No use thinking about him. I'll never see him again. I don't even know his fucking name." Climbing on her bed, she lay down, closed her eyes, and went to sleep.

Joe grabbed some boxes from the box store and headed home. Looking around, he realized there wasn't very much he really wanted to keep. Everything there represented a life he was no longer willing to live. He grabbed his favorite pans from the kitchen, his set of knives and a few utensils he preferred, then laughed to himself when he realized the box wasn't even half-full. Setting it on the table, he headed to his bathroom, took what he wanted, then walked to his closet. He had three suitcases full and that was it.

Shaking his head, he pulled out his phone and called Jason.

"Hey, man," Jason answered. "What's up?"

"Yeah, I've decided, you can just have my place. There isn't anything here that I really want. Just don't destroy it. One day, I might want to sell it. I've already packed the shit I want, so the rest is yours."

"No shit. Thanks, man. Do you know if Al is selling his place? Ben wanted to know."

"You'd have to ask him. This place has four bedrooms. Why don't you guys bunk together?"

Jason laughed. "No. I don't want to listen to our baby brother fucking some random chick, nor do I want him to hear me. Hey, can I ask you something personal?"

"Sure, I'm not sure I'm the guy to be asking, but go ahead."

"Have you ever crossed the line and fucked a client?"

"Totally unethical. No, I haven't. Why?"

"This chick, Veronica Holloway, man, she is so fucking fine she gets me hard every fucking time I look at that ass of hers."

"Listen, man, crossing that line is the single most unethical thing you can do. Your job is to protect her, not fuck her. Don't think that way. Don't ever think that way."

"Haven't you ever thought about it?"

"I have, yeah. But when someone trusts you to keep them safe, crossing that line just makes you a scum bag. No one has ever crossed that line, Jason."

"Al did."

"Al also quit right after, and he is married to her. So, don't go doing some stupid shit like that. I just handed you a multi-million-dollar company to run. Keep your fucking dick in your pants. Having a relationship while doing this job isn't an option. Mike is a personal friend of mine. If you fuck his daughter, that's on you, but you will destroy the reputation of the company and have to deal with Mike. Stand down. If you can't control yourself, put one of the guys in charge of her."

"Yeah, you're right. She has been beaten up pretty badly. I had the guy arrested. Fucker jacked her right in front of me. I thought he broke her jaw the way she crumpled like a rag doll. I mean, the chick isn't tall, and she is far from thin. I felt bad for her. I wanted to grab her and hold her, make her feel safe."

"I fucking hate guys like that. I know what you mean about wanting to wrap her in your arms. But don't go there. Listen, I'm waiting on the lawyers so I can sign everything, so you'll be in charge, but then I'm out. Like I said, I'm taking the cabin. We should have a drink before I head out."

"Sounds like a plan, just give me a call. And thanks, brother, for the advice. As always, you're right. She is off limits. Oh, here she comes. Gotta go."

Jason hung up and Joe just shook his head. "Fucking idiot." Joe went about packing his truck up with all his shit. He was driving it back to the cabin. When he finished loading boxes, the lawyers called. The paperwork was ready.

He called Jason and told him to meet him there. Then he was heading out.

Two hours later, the business was Jason's and Joe was free. "Why don't we go grab a drink before you head out? Ben said Holloway's daughter wanted to go out. They're at some club downtown."

"Yeah, I'll go with you. But I'm only having one then heading out after. I've got a long road to travel."

"You're driving?"

"I told you I was out. I'm going to need my truck."

Jason told him where they were going, and they left. Joe needed to stop at the bank and grab some cash. When he walked into the bar, he found a seat close to the door. Jason saw him and came over. They sat there having a drink and talking. Joe got up to use the restroom. "When I come back, I'll give you the apartment keys and the access code to the alarm system."

Making his way through the bar, he headed to the bathroom. As he was washing his hands, a man walked in swearing. "Fucking fat ass bitch." Joe looked in the mirror at the guy. He was stumbling drunk, pissing all over the place and bitching about some girl. Joe just shook his head and walked out, going back to Jason.

"Listen, man, I'm out of here. I'm too old for this shit." Pulling his keys to his building and apartment out of his pocket, he handed them to Jason. "The code is mom's birthday, year included. Don't destroy the company." Leaning in, he said, "Keep your fucking dick in your pants."

Jason laughed. "Don't worry, brother, this chick has enough problems. Fucking me isn't going to help her."

He slapped his brother on the back. "I'll call you in a few weeks." Turning, he started to walk out when he heard someone scream, he watched the drunk guy from the bathroom dragging some woman through the bar, with a gun in his hand. People were running all over the place. Joe's eyes zeroed in on the gun. He watched in horror as Jason stepped in front of him, and the guy raised his hand and shot Jason in the shoulder. Joe went to move, but when the guy flung the woman he was dragging, so she was in front of him as a shield, he froze. It was the woman from the cabin. Stepping back, he waited for the guy to walk toward him, watching the woman try to get away from him. The guy raised the hand with the gun to hit her in the face.

"No!" Joe yelled, charging at him, catching the guy off guard. Joe hit him as hard as he could in the face, knocking him out cold, and grabbed Roni, pulling her into his arms, moving her away from the asshole on the floor. Looking at the bartender, he yelled, "Call nine-one-one!"

Looking at Roni, he asked, "Are you all right?" She just stood there looking at him. "Roni?" He shook her. "Are you all right?"

She nodded at him. He let her go, moving to the guy on the floor. He picked up his gun, shoving it in his pants, then moved to his brother who was getting up.

"Fucker shot me," Jason said.

"Are you all right?"

"Yeah, fucking hurts. Is she all right?"

Joe turned to look at her. She was fucking beautiful standing there in a pair of jeans and a t-shirt, not one ounce of makeup on her face, her lip tucked between her teeth. He looked back at his brother. "That's your job?"

"Yeah, Veronica Holloway."

"That's Mike's daughter?"

"Yeah, why? Fuck."

Joe stood and looked at her. *Holy shit.* The guy he knocked out was starting to move, so Joe punched him again. Stepping over him, he moved to Roni. Her eyes stayed glued to his. He reached up to touch the bruise on her cheek. "This is the fucker who hurt you? This is why you were in the woods?"

Her eyes moved to look at the guy on the floor, then back to Joe. Nodding, her eyes locked with his again. "Come on, I'll take you home." Turning, he looked at Jason. "I'll take her home. Get to the hospital. I'll wait to leave until morning."

Jason nodded and watched his brother wrap his arm around Veronica in a very possessive way, pulling her into his side, almost as if he knew her. They walked out the door as the police were walking in.

Joe stopped. "The fucker shot my brother. Here's his gun." He pulled the gun out from the back of his jeans. "Put him away."

"Sorry, Joe. I'm going to need your statement."

"I'll be down there in an hour. I need to get this woman home."

The cop looked at her. "Miss Holloway, I'm sorry but he made bail."

She just nodded to him. Joe led her out to his truck. Opening the door, he lifted her up into it. He stood there looking at her. "I just want you to know, it mattered to me, what we did." She just looked at him.

He stepped back and shut her door. *Jesus fucking Christ.* Climbing into his truck, he started it and headed out to Holloway's house.

"I don't want to go home," she said softly.

"I need to take you home. I have to meet my brother at the hospital and then go to the station."

"Jason is your brother? Your name is Blackshaw? I didn't know what your name was."

Joe didn't say anything to her. He just drove out to her father's house. Pulling up, he helped her out of the truck and walked her into the house. Her father met them in the front hall.

"Joe, what the hell happened? Ben called and said your brother was shot."

"Yeah, I'm on my way to the hospital. Six of my guys are outside, but that fucker is on his way to jail. She should be safe for the night."

"Now that your brother is hurt, are you staying on to protect her?"

"Mike, I told you I'm out. Jason is the boss now. I was just having a drink with him before I headed out. My truck is packed."

"Joe, he got his hands on her. She can't live in hiding."

"Mike, he's going to jail. He shot my brother in a crowded club. If a judge lets him out, call me. I'll leave my phone on. It'll take me a few days to get where I'm going, so I can always jump on a plane. She'll be fine." He looked at her as she stood by the stairs. Her eyes never left his. He nodded to her and walked out the door.

Fuck! She is Mike's daughter. Fuck! He got in his truck and sat there looking at the front door. Could he leave? Should he leave? He had to leave. Mike wouldn't understand. Hell, he didn't understand. The only thing he knew was that she felt right in his arms. Shaking his head, he started his truck and left.

Roni stood there lost in her own head. *He's Joe Blackshaw and he's leaving. A friend of her father's. God, he is so fucking beautiful, and he saved me.* When he turned to look at her, she saw in his eyes that he didn't want to leave her. But he walked out the door.

"Are you all right?" her father asked.

She just nodded and went upstairs. She wanted to know all there was to know about him. But she couldn't ask her father. Joe was her father's friend. "Holy shit." She let him fuck her, twice. Climbing on her bed, she sat in the middle. Closing her eyes, she relived those fifteen minutes she'd spent at his mercy. Licking her lips, she smiled, wondering what it would be like to spend a night with him, a day, a few days. Shaking her head, she lay down, closing her eyes. She just wanted this all to be over so she could move on with her life.

Her thoughts were still on Joe and the way he manhandled her, and then his kindness and concern when he found her in the woods. "Maybe he's not a bastard. Maybe he is a nice guy." She knew she was dreaming, making him something she was sure he wasn't. He was a badass professional security guy. A man who can, could, and probably had killed people.

~

Joe went to the hospital to check on Jason, then to the police station to give his report. When he was finished, he headed back to his apartment. He couldn't get her out of his head. She was fucking stunning without all that makeup on. His clothes came off, and he lay in bed, her eyes boring into his mind. His cock grew harder as the minutes passed. There was something about her, some kind of connection between them; he could feel it. She wasn't a quick fuck for release, definitely not a quick fuck.

Rolling over, he forced himself to sleep.

CHAPTER FOUR

The ringing phone woke Joe. Rolling over, he grabbed it off the charger. "Yeah," he griped.

"Joe, Mike Holloway. I just wanted to update you on the guy who shot your brother. He's in jail, facing attempted murder charges."

"Good." He needed to know how she was. "How's your daughter doing?"

"She went to her room and hasn't come out since. She spends the majority of her time up there. Last night was a rare occasion for her. One of her friends asked her to dinner. Although, considering what happened, I think Veronica was set up. With your brother out of commission, would you reconsider staying to see this through?"

As much as he wanted to stay, he knew he couldn't. "Mike, with this asshole in jail, she is going to be fine. Ben is a dead shot. Jason isn't out of commission. I stopped by the hospital last night, and he's fine. They can handle this. Don't forget there are six guys outside your house twenty-four seven. Maybe it would be best if you just kept her at home until this was over."

Mike laughed as Joe sat up. "You don't know my daughter. But, then again, I don't know her very well anymore. I still can't believe I wanted her to marry that asshole. He's been beating the shit out of her for nearly a year and she never said a word. Why do they do that?"

"You're asking the wrong man."

"Damn, sorry about that. Listen, thanks for saving her last night. You take care of yourself."

"Thanks, Mike. I'll keep in touch with Jason for you, just to make sure everything is going well. You take care of yourself."

"You too. Enjoy your retirement."

Joe disconnected the call. "Fuck."

Three hours later, he was heading to the cabin. His life was all his now. No more business, no more anything. He just couldn't get her out of his mind. Why would anyone stay? He needed to put her out of his head. It would never be anything more than what it was, a fifteen-minute interlude. Laughing aloud, he berated himself. "Yeah, a fifteen-minute interlude that fucking derailed me." He couldn't let it go on any longer. Time and distance were the only way to settle this.

When Roni finally came downstairs, her father informed her that Tony was in jail for attempted murder and attempted kidnapping. She knew she should have felt a sense of satisfaction but, somehow, she knew this wasn't over. He would get out and he would come for her.

"Thanks, Daddy, but I know it's not over. Are you sure it's all right if I stay here? I need to figure out what the hell to do with my life. I should get a job or something."

He smiled at her. "Sweetheart, you just spent the last year of your life being hurt by the man you love. Taking time to heal from that isn't an outrageous thing."

"I know, but I just think maybe I should leave L.A., maybe go somewhere that no one knows me. I was thinking about maybe going to Chicago or New York."

"How about we wait until all of this is settled?"

She nodded, knowing he was right. "Okay, Daddy. Thank you."

Time moved forward for Roni at a snail's pace. Tony had been charged with assault with a deadly weapon, attempted murder, and attempted kidnapping. The judge didn't grant him bail, so he was in jail awaiting trial.

Weeks had passed, and Roni still just sat in her room. One afternoon, her father came up to see her.

"Veronica, I'm worried about you. You've been up here for weeks, sweetheart. What is going on?"

"To be honest, Dad, I'm not sure. Mostly, I'm trying to avoid Mother. She just can't get over Tony. Why is she like that? Why does she treat me so badly all the time?"

"I don't know. Listen, Tony's trial is coming up, and I spoke to the judge. You can go in and give your testimony, that way you won't need to be in court. Then, why don't you go up to the cabin for a while? You seem to be the only one who enjoys that place. I know, as a family, we haven't been up there since you were a child."

"Daddy, as much as I would love to go, is that the best idea?"

"Sweetheart, Jason and Ben haven't been here for almost a month now. You are perfectly safe. You don't even go out to the garden, and you need fresh air. Winter is coming soon. Why don't you go up there? I'll arrange everything."

She nodded, knowing she didn't want to go anywhere. She wanted to wait for Joe to come back. He had to come back eventually. He owned the security company, didn't he?

Two days later, she was on the family plane headed to Minnesota. Her father had the house stocked with food and arranged for a driver to pick her up and drive her out. He was right; she needed to feel something. Get some fresh air, clear her head, and get over fucking Joe Blackshaw. He didn't come for her, so she was just what she believed her to be, a one-time thing.

So many times, Joe wanted to go back and get her, go back and make sure she was all right. He had called Jason and Mike a few times. But, once Jason stopped watching over her, there was no excuse.

Weeks had passed, and he still couldn't get her out of his mind. The way her eyes bore into his stopped his heart. But did he really want to be bothered with a woman who was so obviously fucked up? The more he thought about it, the more he believed that is exactly what he wanted.

He was checking his emails and saw one from Jason. He needed to go back for that fucking guy's trial. Something he would gladly do. Maybe then, Roni would have some peace of mind and could go on with her life. So, he sent Jason an email and told him to send the plane, only to discover it was already in Minneapolis.

Joe packed a bag and headed out. He was going to make sure this asshole paid big time. Maybe, with a little luck, he would get twenty years.

Roni slept when she got to the house. She believed she was depressed. Being alone probably wasn't the best choice, but she was afraid all the time. Her friends abandoned her, and her mother wouldn't let up with the relentless badgering.

When she woke, she ate then decided to go for a walk. She hadn't been outside in any real capacity in a very long time. Tony had made her a prisoner. She was terrified all the time of doing something that would set him off. Walking along the little creek, she tried to remember when it all started, but she couldn't pinpoint a time, just that it had happened nearly once a week. If he was in town from D.C., it would happen more often.

But it was over now. She had given her statement to a court reporter, and his trial was set to start soon. Her father would make sure he went to jail. He did, after all, shoot Jason Blackshaw, and from what Roni could tell, the Blackshaw brothers were men you didn't mess with. As she walked, she remembered the nearly forgotten fifteen minutes she gave herself to a complete stranger. When she looked up, she was standing in his yard along the creek, her eyes glued to the doors on the deck. *Is he here? Is this where he disappeared to?* Fighting with herself not to go up and knock, she kept walking.

It just wasn't meant to be anything other than what it was. He was her father's friend, which meant he was much older than her. Not to mention, her father would probably have a stroke.

Her life was her own now. She was there to figure out what to do with it. L.A. wasn't an option for her, and D.C. was not a place she wanted to live. She had gone to college to be a teacher, so maybe she would do that. Maybe there was a school in Minnesota that she could teach at. Nodding, she decided that was what she would do. Give herself a few weeks to become her again, instead of this sheltered basket case of a victim she had become.

When Joe landed, Jason was there to pick him up. "You look good."

Joe chuckled. "Thanks, so do you."

"Looks like retirement is just what you needed."

"You know, I think you are right. I actually sleep at night, which is something I haven't done in a long time. When you learn to survive on four hours here and there, it wears on you. I'm sleeping like eight to ten hours a night."

Jason laughed. "Tell me about it. Not that I'm complaining. You and Al built a great company, and I couldn't be happier that you gave it to me."

"But?"

"The hours suck, Joe, and the paperwork sucks, but the pay is more than anyone could ask for."

"Just don't get stupid. Put it away so, when it's your time to retire, you have more than enough to survive on without having to work another day."

"Oh, I've been putting it away." Pulling up to Joe's old place, they went in. "The trial starts tomorrow, nine a.m."

"Good, the sooner this is over, the sooner I can go back home. I love it there. So quiet."

"Have you found a woman yet?"

Shaking his head, Joe smiled at him, knowing he had but there was nothing he could do about it. "Nope, and I'm fine with that."

Getting serious, Jason asked him, "Listen, that night this fucker shot me, did I see what I thought I saw?"

"What do you mean?"

"Was there something going on with you and Veronica?"

Joe stood there looking at his brother then shook his head. "Nope. You know where that came from. You know how I feel about assholes who hit. Just had a flashback; that's all it was."

Jason looked at his brother. He knew better, and his response was bullshit because none of them knew their sister was being beaten by her husband. "Well, you didn't cross the line if there was."

"There wasn't, so this conversation is over. I'm going to take a shower and hit the hay. We have a big day tomorrow."

"Yeah, I'll see you in the morning."

Joe took his bag and headed into the spare room. This was no longer his house. He took a shower and crawled into bed. Lying there on his back staring at the ceiling, he couldn't get her out of his mind. He was here in the city, and so was she. He would see her at the trial. "Fuck." He wished she wasn't Mike's daughter. He really respected the man, and this would definitely not be the best idea. But at least he could see her again. Smiling, he closed his eyes with thoughts of that perfect ass in his mind and crashed.

Morning came too fast for Joe. He wanted to stay in the slumber of lust. When he woke, he was rock hard, and not with his usual morning erection. This one was fueled by his dreams of her. He wasn't a man who jacked off, but he'd had this erection for weeks now. Nothing seemed to sedate him.

Stepping into the hot shower, his erection was so hard, so big his head was swollen to a deep red and touching his stomach. "Fuck it." He soaped up his hand and grabbed a hold of it, stroking slowly. Stepping back, he leaned against the tile, his eyes closed, his mind locked on those fifteen minutes of pure heaven he'd spent with her. It didn't take much before his stomach tightened and he exploded. The relief was intense, but the lust was still there. He had it bad for this woman. Never had he felt like this about anyone.

Chuckling when he looked down at the cum on the floor, he wondered if this was what it was like for Al. He washed and got out. Grabbing his phone, he called Al.

"Hey, brother, what's up?"

"Is there any way we can have a private conversation? I need to talk to you about some shit."

"Yeah, hold on." Joe could hear him talking to Becca. Then he heard the screen door shut. "Okay, what's up?"

"I think I'm fucked."

Al laughed. "What's her name?"

"Listen, you can't say a fucking word about this. I had no idea what the fuck was going on. I quit, as you know, and I was up at the cabin. Well, I was sitting there on the deck trying to decompress and out of nowhere came this screaming. So, you know me, I was off to investigate. Well, it was this high maintenance chick in the woods screaming and crying."

Al busted out laughing. "You and a high maintenance chick? Jesus, Joe, what the hell?"

"It wasn't like that, asshole. Shut the fuck up and let me finish."

"By all means, I want to hear this."

"When I realized she was just being a drama queen, I walked away. A bit later, she showed up at the cabin dressed to fucking kill. The chick walked through the fucking woods in high heels. So, you know me, I told her how it was, and she huffed off the deck and stormed away, throwing some kind of hissy fit. About an hour later, I was sitting with my eyes closed and I couldn't get her out of my fucking mind. She is so fucking beautiful it scared the shit out of me. So, I headed out to find her, only she was on her way back to the cabin. She'd changed her shoes into boots, washed all the makeup off her face, and changed her shirt. But damn if she didn't have on the tightest pair of fucking jeans."

Al was laughing. "You fucked her, didn't you?"

"Man did I ever. She was fucking bare as a hardwood floor. Her ass, well, yeah. She was fucking magnificent. The problem is that I fucking kissed her, and she was the sweetest thing I ever tasted. We went a second round. She didn't make a sound, not one moan, not one grunt, and when we were done, she rolled over, got dressed, and left without saying a word."

"Your kind of girl, wasn't she?"

Joe chuckled. "Perfect."

"But?"

"But something didn't feel right, so I went after her. Found her in the woods hysterical. So, I brought her back to the cabin, but she just left once she calmed down."

"So, what's the problem?"

"I can't get her out of my fucking head. It's been weeks. But there's more. Mike Holloway wanted me to protect his princess of a daughter, but I declined, and Jason took the job. Well, I had stopped to have a drink with him before I left. Turns out the princess he was hired to protect was, in fact, her. She's Mike's daughter."

Al busted out laughing. "No fucking way. What the hell, Joe? You gave us shit all the time about crossing the line. I fucking quit my job because I did it. Well, that and I'm sure Bec wouldn't have let me work anymore. But you crossed more than one line here. You know that, right?"

"Yeah, I fucking know that, better than anyone."

"Man, you fucked your friend's daughter. How do you even come back from that?"

"That's the thing, man. I don't want to come back from that. Al, I think I have some serious feelings for this girl. Mike is going to kill me when he finds out."

"Why does he have to find out? You aren't ever going to see her again."

"I know you're right. I know it makes sense to just forget it. But I can't, like you with Becca. You knew what you were doing was wrong, but you couldn't stop yourself. That's how it is with me."

"Joe, man, she is Mike's daughter. That's a line you never cross."

"But I did, and I have zero regrets. Man, when I looked into her eyes, I was gone. I mean seriously gone. I need to talk to Mike. I need to tell him what the hell happened, and how I feel. Just like you did when you crossed it with Bec."

"You do know he is going to go batshit crazy, right?"

He chuckled. "I know. But it's the right thing to do."

"Well, at least you weren't really protecting her when it happened."

"Yeah, there's that."

"Do yourself a favor."

"What's that?"

Al took a deep breath. "Think of it as if your friend was sitting you down to tell you that he fucked your daughter and now he has a thing for her."

"Fuck. I can't do that. I can't tell him. Hell, I'll probably never see her again. This is going to kill him. I know because it's killing me."

"Listen, Joe, you are a hell of a man. It's not like you're some low life who took advantage of his only daughter."

Joe laughed. "That's the problem. I did take advantage of her. Big time. But fuck, if she didn't take a bit of my fucking heart and soul with her when she left."

"You've got it bad. I'm glad."

"Fuck you. I think I just need to get laid. Thanks for listening. We are due in court."

"Good luck. Make that fucker pay for shooting our little brother."

"That's the plan. Tell Bec I said hi, and you take care, brother."

"You do the same."

Joe disconnected the call and headed out to the kitchen to get something to eat. Jason was already in the middle of cooking. He stood there looking at him. Jason gave him his famous 'you are in some deep shit' look.

"We didn't get a chance to talk before you left, and this isn't a conversation I wanted to have on the phone. But, Joe, we need to talk."

Closing his eyes, he took a deep breath. Looking at his little brother, he cracked a slight smile. "Not sure I want to have this conversation."

"Too bad. What did I see at that bar?"

"I have no idea. You tell me." Joe wasn't giving anything up. Jason was going to have to pry it out of him.

"Did you sleep with her? Are you sleeping with her? Is that why you refused the case?"

Joe grabbed a cup of coffee while Jason was questioning him. "Yes, no, and no."

"Fuck, Joe, she's Mike's only daughter. He's your friend."

"I fucking know that. At the time, I didn't have a clue who she was. The last time I saw her, she was a little girl. I didn't know it was her until we were in that bar."

"What are you going to do? Have you seen her since?"

"I don't have a fucking clue what I'm going to do. I know I should tell Mike, but we go way back and I'm not so sure he's going to be my friend when I do tell him. No, I haven't seen her since. It was just a one-time thing that happened."

"I saw your face, your eyes. It's more than that and you know it."

He hadn't realized how transparent he was. Shaking his head, Joe reluctantly told him, "She got to me. It happened a long time ago though. I'm sure she has more than forgotten about me."

Jason handed him a plate of food. "You're fucked. You know that, right?"

"Yeah, I know. Now, can we drop it, please? If I hadn't watched that bastard shoot you, I wouldn't be here. I wouldn't have to face her or Mike."

Jason looked at him and smiled. "Neither of them will be there. Well, Mike might, but Veronica gave her testimony in private to the judge with a court reporter there. It will be read to the jury. She's in bad shape over all of this. Mike said the guy had been beating the shit out of her for over a year. As far as I know, she hasn't left the house since that night. Her friend set her up when he got to her at the club. Mike said she just sits in her room all day doing nothing."

Joe's stomach rolled with disgust. His heart warmed fully, and there wasn't a fucking thing he could do about it. Hearing this only made him know why she'd been so quiet, why she was crying and screaming. She was completely alone. Joe knew her mother; the woman was a stone-cold bitch. The biggest society snob he had ever met. She even tried to fuck him years ago. Joe hated her.

They ate without saying another word. Joe just wanted to get the fuck out of there and go back to Minnesota. They dressed and headed to court. Joe was called to testify, where he told his account of what he saw. Looking at the fucker sitting there with a smug look on his face, Joe wanted to punch him again.

When the day was done, he spoke to the district attorney about leaving. He didn't want to be there. He didn't want to see Mike or take the chance of seeing Roni. He was told he wasn't needed anymore, so they headed back to Jason's.

"Listen, man, I'm going back to the cabin. I can't take the chance of running into her, or into Mike. I need to stay as far away from here as I can get. Don't tell him where I am, all right?"

"I won't say a word. Thanks, man, for coming and doing this."

"Yeah, well, if the fucker gets off, call me."

"He isn't getting out. Take care, brother, and don't be a stranger. Mom wants us all home for Christmas. Al and Becca are coming, so your ass better be there."

Joe laughed. "Yeah, I'll be there. Take care."

The brothers hugged, and Joe headed back to the airport, then back to Minnesota.

CHAPTER FIVE

Roni walked the property each day for a while. She took the car and wandered into town looking for the school. Maybe she could apply for a substitute teaching position. The school didn't take long to find. They were, in fact, looking for one after the holidays, so she could start teaching second grade then.

Feeling better about herself, for the first time in a very long time, she decided to treat herself to lunch at the diner. She met a few people, who were all very sweet to her. She told them that she was the new second-grade substitute teacher. Everyone seemed pleased and happy about it.

When the afternoon was all said and done, she found herself walking along the creek, finally a bit settled down from the past year of her life. The fear was a constant in her mind, in her actions. She was still struggling with her mother and the reality that she hated her. *How can a woman hate her own child?*

As she strolled along the creek's edge, she happened to look up, her heart stopping in her chest. Joe Blackshaw stood less than ten feet from her with his chiseled jaw, his broad shoulders, and his stoic expression. She didn't know what to do. Why now? Her eyes darted around looking for an escape. Her cheeks flushed with the guilt of her thoughts concerning him. Turning, she just walked away. She could feel her hands shaking, hear her heart beating in her ears. "Oh my God." Her voice was so soft only she could hear it.

Joe had done all he could to forget her, to move forward. It took all he had not to stop by Mike's house, knowing he would be in D.C., hoping to see Roni. It bothered him that she had shut herself away, but he understood. The imagination he had concerning her abuse was the same he learned to deal with when his sister was murdered. How do you not know someone is being so terribly abused? So many questions he had asked himself over the years. The same questions replayed in his mind again, making his heart heavy over the past few months. This girl, this woman, was embedded deeper in his heart and mind than he wanted.

Sitting on his deck, he needed to take Al's advice and just forget it. Mike wouldn't understand. Hell, he didn't understand. He wouldn't understand if it was his daughter and his friend.

Getting all wound up and pissed off, he pushed up out of the chair and stepped off the deck. He needed to walk this shit off, which he knew was a lie; he was heading to the house up the way to see if that's where she'd come from. He didn't want to admit how badly he hoped she'd be there, but he just wasn't sure it's where she went, where she was.

As he started down the path, a path that hadn't been there a month before, he saw someone walking toward him. His feet stopped moving, and his breath hitched in his chest as his eyes adjusted. When she picked her head up, it felt like the world stopped moving. There was no sound, nothing moved. It was just him and her. He could see the wonder in her eyes, then the sadness, and, out of nowhere, the fear.

He couldn't move. Joe wanted to grab her and pull her to him, but he didn't move. Was he really seeing her, or was it just his mind playing games with him? When she turned and walked away, Joe didn't know what to do. He wanted to go after her, but her body language warned him not to. So, he just stood there and watched her perfect ass walk away.

When she disappeared into the woods, a small smile crept across his face. *She's here. She's safe.* That's all that mattered to him. At least, that's what he told himself. Turning, he headed back to his cabin, knowing they should talk. They would need to discuss what happened.

Plopping down in his chair, he stared out at the water. He had never wanted to talk to a woman more than he did now. He wanted so much more than to talk, but in his heart, he knew it could never happen again. He knew she was completely off limits, his friend's daughter. "What the fuck."

Pushing up, he headed in the house to grab his phone. He needed to talk to Al. Dialing the number, he headed out to the creek.

"Yeah," Al said.

Joe chuckled. "Did I catch you at a bad time?"

"No, we're at the beach. It's getting cold out so our time is limited. What's up? Hey, did you testify?"

"Yeah, then I got the hell out of there. I really wasn't sure I was going to enjoy retirement, but you know, I am liking this."

Al busted out laughing. "It definitely has its advantages. You all right?"

Joe let out a deep breath before responding. "No, not really." He turned to look down the path, and standing about twenty feet away was Roni. "Man, I need to call you back."

"You sure?"

"Yep." Joe disconnected the call.

His eyes didn't move from hers. He could hear his heartbeat in his ears. She just stood there, not moving, staring at him. He wanted to move but was frozen. She was the one who moved toward him. He didn't even blink as he watched her take step after step. When she was about five feet away, she stopped, looking up at him.

Her eyes were so green, the whites glossy, the rims a bit red. She'd been crying. Joe wanted to reach for her, to touch her, to kiss her, to hold her. He wanted to make her feel fucking safe, but he didn't move.

They stood there, five feet apart from one another, just looking in each other's eyes. Neither of them moved or spoke; they just stood there. Joe tried to see past the pain, while Veronica tried to see past her anger.

She took a deep breath. "Why?" Her voice was soft. "Why didn't you say something to me?"

"I didn't know what to say." His words were kind, but his eyes filled with anger.

She nodded and turned to walk away. Joe reached out and touched her arm. "Don't," he whispered. "Don't walk away."

"It doesn't matter. You won't follow me. I know that now. It was a mistake coming here." She pulled out of his grip and walked back into the woods.

Joe fought with himself not to go after her. The feeling that zipped up his arm when he touched her shocked him. He wanted her like he wanted his next breath. But she was right; he wouldn't follow her. He couldn't. She was his friend's daughter. Crossing that line again, knowing who she was, was unacceptable. It was a line he couldn't uncross.

Dropping his head when she was out of his sight, he walked back to his cabin and moved to the deck. As he sat in his chair, his eyes bored into the woods. His brain repeatedly told him it was wrong to have these feelings, to have this desire. But his body, his heart was telling his mind to shut the hell up. Would Mike understand? He knew he wouldn't if it was his daughter. He would be out for blood.

Veronica walked slowly through the woods, hoping with all she had that he would follow her. But he didn't. And she knew why. He was her father's friend, and he was older than her, but none of that mattered to her. She wanted him, but even that thought confused her.

He made it perfectly clear that what they'd done was all there would ever be.

She felt the warmth of her tears as they escaped down her cheeks. Her fingers quickly wiped them away as she chastised herself. "I will not cry over him." After walking up the path to the house, she slammed the door and screamed. She felt like such a fool. It was one time, a few fucking minutes of pure bliss, months ago. There shouldn't be any residual feelings toward him. It was what it was, a total lapse in judgment on her part. She shook her head. "If that's all it was, then why do I still want him?" Pushing off the door, she headed to the kitchen to eat. Then she was going to bed. She wanted to sleep the rest of her life away.

Joe sat on his deck for what seemed like hours thinking about her. Thinking about how much he would hate it if she was his daughter. He really needed to get a grip. It was easier knowing she was two thousand miles away, but now, now she was just down the path. His eyes shifted to the woods. He should have spoken to her, made her understand the line he'd crossed. The line that was much bigger now that he knew who she was.

Pushing up, he headed inside to get something to eat. After he went to lay on the bed, he knew he needed to call Al back. Looking at the clock, he realized it was late, so he would call him tomorrow. Picking up his phone, he checked his messages and his emails to see how things were going with the trial. "No news." He dropped his phone onto the bed.

He lay there for hours, unable to sleep, unable to do anything but see visions of her in his mind. Her ass, those incredible tits, and she tasted so sweet to him. Never had a woman tasted that sweet. Before he knew what he was doing, he was out the door, looking at the woods.

"Fuck." He knew he was going to burn in hell. Off the deck he went. As he started up the path, he stopped short when he realized Roni was walking toward him.

She stopped, looking up at him. "I can't stand this anymore. Why didn't you say something? Was it because of my father?"

Joe stepped forward, moving closer to her until he stood less than a foot from her. His hand moved on its own, gently touching her face. "I didn't know who you were, and if I had, that would have never happened."

Her eyes bored into his. "You're a liar." The words were soft, her breath warm on his fingers. "You're a fucking liar."

Joe smiled as his fingers snaked into her hair, pulling it tight against her scalp. "I don't lie," he groaned as he pulled her head back.

"Maybe not, but you are now." So soft her voice.

Joe watched her lick her lips. His mouth slowly and gently came down on hers. He engulfed her soul, taking everything from her in that kiss. He felt it to the core of his being. No woman had ever made him feel like this. Pulling back, he whispered, "So fucking sweet. You taste so fucking sweet." He claimed her mouth again. When he finished, he stepped back, letting her hair go. They just stood there looking at each other. Shaking his head, he turned and walked away, cursing himself for giving in as much as he had. He was giving her mixed messages. He was playing with her, with her emotions. He wasn't that kind of man. He despised women who played games like this.

He stopped walking and turned to look at her. "He wouldn't understand. I know, because if you were my daughter and a man like me wanted you, took from you what I took, I would want the fucker dead."

"You didn't take anything that I didn't willingly give you."

He stepped toward her. "Did you know who I was?" He was angry now.

She shook her head. "No. I just needed to feel wanted. Something I haven't felt in a very long time. I just wanted to feel anything other than the pain that is me."

He stood there trying to rein in his anger. He didn't trust women, and this woman in front of him, well, he wanted her. The lust flowing through his veins was more than he could handle. "I can't do this with you, Veronica."

"My name is Roni. He called me Veronica, and you are not him. Or, are you?" Her question was laced with venom.

A smile crossed his lips. "Oh, sweetheart, I am him. The difference is, the pain is nothing but pleasure." He wanted to scare her, make her back away from him. But she stood there with defiance in her eyes.

As she licked her lips and tucked her bottom lip between her teeth, Joe had to stop the moan. "You wouldn't hurt me like that."

"Don't be so sure of yourself."

"You're not that man, Joe Blackshaw. You and I both know it."

He chuckled. "You don't know a thing about the type of man I am. Go home, Veronica." Turning, he walked away. He didn't stop, even when he slammed the door behind him. He was so pissed off at himself. He should have never kissed her. Now, she was freshly embedded in his soul. He knew he wasn't going to stop wanting her, desiring her. He knew he was going to cross that line.

Walking into the bedroom, he grabbed his phone off the bed and dialed Al.

"Hey, man, is everything all right?"

"Sorry to wake you, brother, but I need to fucking talk to someone before I lose my fucking mind."

"Give me a minute," Al said. Joe could hear him talking to Becca. Then he heard the door shut. "What's going on?"

"Al, fuck, she is here. I fucking kissed her again. Man, I seriously think I have some feelings for this girl. I am in so much fucking trouble."

"Who's there? Veronica?"

"Yeah. What the hell am I going to do?"

Al laughed. "Well, brother, I have never heard you talk like this about a woman before. So, I would say, do what feels like the right thing for you. Listen, not that I am a parent, or that I will ever be a parent, but I think the only thing parents ever want for their children, especially daughters, is for a good man to love them, protect them, and take care of them. Joe, you are a good man, and Mike knows that. I'm sure he will eventually see that you care for her. That you might even be in love with her. Eventually, he will come to terms with it."

Joe didn't say anything for a minute. "Do you think so? I mean, I'm at a loss here. She's like fifteen years younger than me. I'm an old fucking man compared to her."

Al laughed. "Age is only a number. I'm younger than Becca, but do you think that bothers me? Nope, it doesn't. Just let Mike go in this equation. It isn't about Mike. This is about you. Neither of you knew who the other was when you jumped her. So, big deal, now you know. Your feelings aren't any different now that you know, are they?"

"No, man they're not. If anything, they are stronger. The problem is, do I want her more now because I know she is forbidden?"

Al chuckled. "Only you can answer that. But I know you, and I know you don't work like that, and Mike knows that about you. Joe, you've never allowed yourself to get close to a woman. Not since Julia, and that was nearly twenty years ago. You always keep yourself closed off. Man, you are forty-five. Let yourself go. Let yourself love."

Joe swallowed. Was he in love with her? Impossible. "There is no way I'm in love with her. I don't even know her. I spent fifteen minutes fucking the hell out of her, then it was over."

"Well, apparently, it was more than just fucking. Listen, man, my wife is standing on the deck looking at me. I'm outside buck ass naked. Go talk to her, something I know you have never done with a woman outside of business. I'm going to go. Call me tomorrow. Or not."

"Yeah, thanks."

Joe disconnected the call and rested his arms on his thighs. His mind wandered in a million directions at once. Closing his eyes, he could still taste her on his lips, he could still feel her perfect skin on his fingertips. The way her hair felt wrapped around his hand. The sweet smell of her embedded in his nose.

He got up, needing a drink. Hell, he needed her. When he walked out of the kitchen with a beer in his hand, he saw her standing at his door. His body froze. He knew what he was going to do the minute she licked her lips. Setting the beer on the counter, he walked to the door and pulled it open.

She just stood there looking at him. He watched as her shaking hand reached up and she gently placed it on his chest. It was when she blinked that he picked her up, her legs wrapping around him, her mouth crashing down on his, her hands tugging at his hair.

Turning, Joe kicked the door shut and was moving through the cabin to his bedroom. Climbing on the bed, he laid her on her back, their mouths not parting. He gently laid his body over hers, resting his weight on his elbows, her legs still wrapped around him. She tasted so good. He slowed the kiss and took his time tasting her. The gentle swipes of his tongue along hers, the tugs of her lips between his teeth. Her soft and gentle mews. His senses were on overload, his cock harder than fucking stone, but the urgency to fuck her was gone. Something more filled him now. It wasn't that uncontrollable desire to release. It was deeper, much deeper.

Pulling back, he looked at her, his thumb brushing along her swollen lips. "So fucking sweet," he whispered, leaning in to kiss her again. It went on for a good half-hour, the two of them lying in bed in that position just kissing one another. There was no touching, no ripping clothes off one another, just kissing.

As Joe slowed the kiss, pulling back to look at her, her eyes closed. *Fucking beautiful.* She slowly opened her eyes, and he could see the tears building up. Still, he said nothing as they escaped down the sides of her face. Her legs released his hips, and her hand pressed on his chest. He moved off her, rolling onto his side, his hand coming to rest on her stomach.

He watched her wipe the tears from her face, but when she moved to sit up, Joe pressed on her stomach, signaling to her not to move. "Don't run," he said softly.

"I won't. I need to breathe." He released his hand as she raised her body and sat next to him. She pulled her legs up to her chest, wrapping her arms around them.

Joe didn't know what to say, what to do. Sitting next to her, he told her, "Your father isn't going to understand this. Hell, I don't understand this."

"I know, neither do I. With everything that has happened, that is happening, those fifteen minutes we spent in this bed all those months ago seem to have stopped me from thinking or caring about anything but that. With being here again," she turned her head to look at him, "I can't get you out of my head."

"Is that why you're here again? Did you come to find me?" His voice was a bit hard.

She shook her head. "My father made me come here. I had no idea you would be here. I thought you were still in L.A. Don't you have a business to run?"

"I retired. I'm done. Roni, Mike is my friend. He's been my friend for twenty years now. I'm a lot older than you are. I'm not sure he is going to forgive me."

"We haven't done anything. At least, we haven't since you've known I'm his daughter."

Joe chuckled. "Maybe not, but I'm pretty sure we'll cross that line. I've done nothing but think about you since that day. When I saw you in that restaurant with that fucker, everything became very clear to me."

"What is that?"

He just sat there looking at her. He couldn't make himself say the words. This was taboo. Thinking about a relationship with her was taboo. He got up and walked out of the room, leaving her sitting on the bed curled around herself. Before he realized where he was going, he was standing by the creek. She was so deep in him that he couldn't breathe. His lust, his desire to own her was so overpowering that he couldn't think straight. He wasn't thinking straight. Should he go and talk to Mike? Should he cross that line and not care about his friend?

The cracking of a branch caused him to turn his head. He just stood there and watched her walk away. He knew he should follow her, knew he should stop her. But fuck, he was an honorable man. He owed it to his friend to not do this. He had to go talk to Mike first.

He found himself in the house with his keys in his hand. After locking up the house, he walked out. When he got to the city, he called Mike.

"Hey, Mike, it's Joe Blackshaw."

"Well, hello, Joe. How's retirement?"

Joe chuckled. "Not sure yet. Listen, I need to see you. Where are you?"

"D.C., I'll be here until Friday. Is everything all right? I know Veronica is fine because that asshole is still in jail."

"I'll be there in a few hours. Can I come by the house?"

"Sure, sure, I'll let the cook know. I have a meeting to get to now, but I'll see you tonight."

Joe disconnected the call, dialing Al. "Hey, man."

Al chuckled. "Brother, we didn't talk this much when we worked together."

"Fuck you. I'm in serious shit here. I'm on my way to see Mike. I have to tell him because I am going to fuck this all up if I don't."

"Joe, don't do this. Just let it be. If you tell him, he is only going to forbid you from seeing her. You are far away from him, from that life. Just be careful, make it mean something. Don't just use her and toss her aside. I know you. You're my brother, and this woman means something to you. Don't do it."

"I just can't help but think how I would feel."

"My advice is to just let this, whatever it is, turn it into something you can show him is real. Don't go to him with the possibility of something that might happen. If she hasn't told him yet, she isn't going to tell him. Why don't you do yourself a favor?"

"What's that?"

"Stop overthinking this. You need to just let it happen. Stop trying to fix everything. Let yourself live, brother. Let yourself feel and be happy. I've known you my whole life. I don't think you have ever been truly happy with your life. This woman has woken your ass up. Let it be what it will be. Keep Mike in the dark until it turns serious."

Joe sat on the side of the road listening to his brother. He knew he was right. Joe knew he just wanted Mike to tell him no because he was scared. "I'm fucking terrified, Al. For the first time in my life, I'm scared as hell. She has the power to hurt me."

"You have some deep feelings for her. I can hear it in your voice. Stop being miserable. Stop looking for a reason not to be happy. Yes, it's scarier than shit, but once you give in and let yourself feel, there is nothing like the love of a good woman to make you feel shit you never knew was out there."

"I know you're right."

"I am. Now, go get her and quit calling me. Becca thinks you've lost your mind. She wants us to come and stay with you. So, go get your girl, Joe, and don't look back. Let yourself go and feel her."

Joe smiled. "Thanks, Al. Thanks for helping me."

"Not a problem. Now, I'm going to go. All this talk of love makes me want to make love to my wife."

"I love you, man."

"I love you, too. Talk soon."

Joe chuckled and disconnected the call. He dialed Mike again, but he didn't pick up this time, so Joe left him a message saying he wasn't coming and that he would talk to him soon. Turning the truck around, he headed back to the cabin.

As he walked through the woods toward her house, or at least what he believed to be her house, he could feel himself come alive. How was it possible to feel like this, to not know someone but know that that person was right for you? He had a million questions running through his head.

He climbed the stairs and knocked on the door. There was a car parked in front of the garage, so he hoped she was there. He knocked again and again, but there was no answer. "Maybe she's out walking." Turning, he saw the chairs and sat in one. He wasn't going anywhere, not until he had the chance to talk to her.

The sun was going down when he heard the rustling of leaves. His head turned toward the woods and, sure enough, there she was. Her head was down, not paying attention to her surroundings, which for some reason pissed him off. He watched her climb the stairs, walking right past him, still not lifting her head. She opened the door and went inside. Joe didn't move; instead, he counted in his head. Fifteen seconds later, she opened the door and looked at him.

"What are you doing here?" she snapped. "I thought you weren't, or couldn't..." She didn't finish her sentence.

Joe stood. "Fuck it." He stepped toward her, his hands grabbing her by the thighs and lifting her to his chest. "I'm going to burn in hell for this," he said softly as he kissed her.

She didn't fight him; she embraced him. When she pulled back, her eyes were full of wonder. "Why are you doing this? I can't handle this game you're playing."

"I am so conflicted about what I'm feeling, about what I am about to do."

"Tell me," her breath hot on his lips, "what are you about to do?"

His smile slowly grew across his lips. "Something I don't think I've ever done before." His feet moved them into the house. "Where is your room?"

Her eyes stayed on his. "Upstairs, end of the hall." She threaded her fingers through his hair, pulling his head to hers as she kissed him.

Joe didn't move. He stood there holding her, absorbing the heat filling his body. He was rock hard, but for some reason, he had no desire to fuck her into next week. No, he didn't want her hard and fast; he wanted to savor her, to take his time. He wanted, no needed, to feel every inch of her, taste every part of her.

She pulled back. "Tell me, Joe. Tell me what you are about to do."

"I'm about to break my own rule. I'm about to cross a line here." His voice sounded groggy and deep, soft and gentle. He was moving up the stairs. "But I can't stop this." Walking into her room, he moved to the bed and climbed on, sitting her on his thighs. His hands moved to her face then into her hair. "So fucking sweet," he moaned out as he kissed her deeply, slowly.

~

Roni didn't know what the hell had gotten into him, and she didn't care. He was different than before. He was gentler, softer, less aggressive. Tender, almost caring. Pulling back, she waited for his eyes to open. "I don't want this to just be a one-time thing again. I want you, Joe Blackshaw, now and in the foreseeable future."

"Sweetheart, I will be the last and only man you will ever have after today."

She felt like teasing him. "You're so sure of yourself."

Chuckling, he tightened his grip on her hair, pulling her lips right to his. "I will never hurt you. I will never lie to you. I don't play games, and when we are done here, you will belong to me and only me."

Roni swallowed hard. "Okay," she squeaked out, her mind in a complete sense of chaotic euphoria. She was about to commit to this man who she knew nothing about. Panic was moving in. Her hands pressed on his chest, and his grip in her hair lessened as she moved away from him.

"Those words were said to me once before, and with that came the most horrifying year of my life. I gave myself to him. He was the first and only man I'd been with until I met you. I'm not so sure I've recovered from that yet, and I know I'm not ready for it again." Her heart slammed in her chest. She was doing everything not to run from him. He was so beautiful, and she knew he would protect her with his life. But what else was he capable of?

He sat there looking at her. "I'm only the second man you've been with?" She nodded. "Jesus." He moved her off his lap and got off the bed. *Holy fucking shit.* He was pacing the room, pulling his own hair. He stopped and looked at her. She looked terrified. "You let me fuck you into oblivion like that?" It wasn't a question he wanted her to answer, but she nodded her head. "Are you fucking serious?" She nodded again. "No wonder you were so upset," he said a bit softer.

"I was upset because..." She stopped talking.

"Because why, Roni?"

"Because I couldn't believe I'd done that. I hadn't really ended my relationship with him. I walked in the door to find him fucking some girl against my living room wall. I watched him take her bare, and he fucking came buried inside of her. He made me get an implant in my arm, so I wouldn't get pregnant, but he always wore a condom. I did what I did with you because I wanted to hurt him," she shouted as she climbed off the bed.

Joe grabbed her around the waist. "So, what you're saying is, at that moment, you would have fucked anyone?" He could feel her trembling. She was scared, panicky, and he was pretty sure she thought he was going to hurt her. So, he pulled her into his chest, wrapping his other arm across her shoulders, and whispered, "I will never hurt you like that. Never. I am not that kind of man."

"The answer to your question is no. That's not who I am. I felt it, too. I felt the connection. You told me what to expect, so I knew what I was doing. But I felt the connection long before you touched me."

"Why didn't you make a sound?" He was calming down a bit.

"Because he told me that if I made a sound it would be worse for me."

Joe closed his eyes. "Roni, did he rape you?" When she nodded her head, he felt rage like he had never known. "When I did that, did you feel like I was doing that to you?"

"It's what he used to do to me, only he would beat the shit out of me before, and usually after, too, because I would try and get away from him. No, with you, it was freeing."

"Fuck." His voice was so soft he wasn't sure he said what he did. "That explains why you said what you said. Roni, I am sorry I scared you."

She turned in his arms, shaking her head. "No, you didn't scare me. You freed me. What we did gave me the strength to go back and tell my father what he was doing. It gave me the strength not to go back again."

Joe wrapped his arms around her, pulling her into his embrace. His breath caught in his chest when she wrapped her arms around him. His mind was so confused. He couldn't take from her like he wanted, and he wouldn't, not yet. She was still so broken inside. She needed caring and strength, not arrogant ravishing.

"Hey." He pulled back, looking at her. "Why don't you pack a few things and come stay with me at the cabin for a few days? Let me take care of you."

She smiled a sweet smile. "I don't need you to take care of me, Joe. I'm doing all right now. I'm learning to deal with the demons that come for me in the night. They come less and less as each night passes."

"I want you to come and hang out with me. Let me help you put them to rest."

Smiling, she nodded, and Joe let out his breath. Watching her move around the room, throwing her clothes and girl things in a bag, made him smile. He had no clue what sort of things a woman needed, but he was willing to find out. More than willing to find out.

Looking at him, she said, "What's the grin for?"

Chuckling, he said, "I've never asked a woman to stay with me before. I was just thinking that I have no clue what a woman needs to survive, and watching you pack your bag just made me feel good. No biggie." She shocked the hell out of him when she busted out laughing. He was baffled. "What?"

"Never?" She giggled.

"No. Now come on." He put on his mean man voice, which just made her giggle more. He reached out, taking her bag in one hand and her hand in the other, and pulled her along with him as her laughter filled the house.

CHAPTER SIX

Together they walked through the woods. When they came out into the clearing, Joe pulled her behind him. There was a bear at the creek. "Don't move," he whispered. Letting go of her hand, he pulled his gun from the back of his jeans. Handing her the bag, he stepped back a step, and when Roni followed him, she stepped on a branch. The crack of the wood sounded like a gunshot in the silence, causing the bear to look up.

Joe froze. He didn't want to shoot the damn thing, but he raised his hand anyway. They stood there, the bear and Joe staring at one another. He watched as the bear sniffed the air. His heart stopped when the bear turned his body toward them, but then it turned and walked back into the woods.

His hand reached back, and Roni put hers in his. Slowly, they made it to the deck before either of them breathed easily again. As he opened the door, moving her into the cabin, he said rather forcefully, "That is why you don't go walking around the woods alone."

"I didn't know there were bears up here," she snapped back at him.

Spinning her around, he grabbed her arms. "Not only are there bears, but there are bobcats, cougars, and wolves. So, no more wandering around in the woods alone."

She smiled at him. "You're pretty bossy."

He couldn't help the smile that appeared on his lips. "You have no idea how bossy I am. Promise me you won't wander off alone. Wolves travel in packs."

She smiled back at him. "Okay! I promise, Mr. Bossy Man."

Joe let her go and turned to close the huge wooden doors across the glass doors, sliding a huge bolt into place. He moved to the windows and did the same to each of them. Then he walked to the back door, closing the huge wooden interior door into place and securing it.

"Jesus, this place is like Fort Knox."

"He knows we are here. He will be back. They aren't stupid, and killing one isn't what I want to do. This is where he lives. He should be getting ready to hibernate for the winter, so I'm sure he is looking for a big meal to tide him over. I just don't want it to be you or me." He walked up to her, running his finger down her jaw, tilting her head up. "I've got plans for you and me, and they don't include death."

He smiled as she swallowed. "Oh?"

"Yeah, oh. Come on, I'll show you where you can put your things."

She followed him into the bedroom. "The closet is there, and this is the bathroom." He went to the windows and closed the wooden shutters, bolting them into place. "Make yourself at home. I have some more windows to lock up."

Roni stood there watching him walk out of the room. "Damn," she whispered to herself. He was fucking huge compared to Tony. Broad shoulders, solid muscle, and sin on two legs. Licking her lips, she turned and walked to the closet, where she took her things from her bag and put them on the bench.

As she walked out of the closet, on her way to the bathroom, she was stopped short by the man leaning against the door frame. Her smile set him in motion, her bag hitting the floor as he picked her up, moving them against the wall. His mouth crashed down on hers the instant her back touched the wood.

Never had she felt this desired, this excited. Dragging her fingers through his hair, digging her nails into his scalp, she tightened her grip. His tongue probed deeper, her breath hinging in her lungs as his grip on her thighs tightened. Her core heated. She wanted this man. She wanted him like nothing she'd ever known.

Pulling out of the kiss, Joe looked at her. "So fucking sweet," he whispered as he kissed her again. When her hands tightened in his hair, he moved them off the wall to the bed. With her securely on his thighs, he let her go, moving his hands up and taking her shirt with them. As he pulled it over her head, they separated. His eyes moved down her body.

She was wearing a sheer black bra. Licking his lips, he knew she was wearing black panties to match. His eyes moved back up to meet the wonder in hers, and he smiled, his fingers unhooking the clasp between her breasts. He nearly came in his jeans when her breasts were freed. When she was lying on her back, he hadn't realized how big they were. He couldn't stop himself from cupping them. He had big hands, and they overflowed his grip. When he ran his thumbs over her already hard nipples, he heard her moan.

"I want to hear your pleasure. Don't hold back."

She smiled at him. "So sure that you can make me scream?"

He chuckled. "So sure." Dipping his head down to lave her hard nipples, he felt her hair on his hand as her head fell back. Sliding his hand up, he fisted it, pulling her body back with her head and laying her on the bed. His mouth never left her nipple. When he clamped his teeth down for a gentle but sharp nip, her hips pressed into him and her back arched. Pushing up, he managed to scoot back so he could look at her. The bruises were gone, her skin nearly white as snow. Joe's need to touch her had his breathing on a scale he had never experienced. He was so hard, but the urgency to release wasn't as strong as his desire to taste her. Leaning in, he drew her taut nipple into his mouth, circling his tongue around it. He felt like he was in heaven. Her nearly silent mews had him aching to hear more. As he pulled back, releasing her nipple, her eyes slowly opened, her tongue sliding across her lips as his eyes slowly drank her in.

Joe's fingers moved down her stomach to her jeans. Slowly, he popped the button, his eyes on hers, then tugged down the zipper. Pulling the material apart, his eyes moved down to see the black lace panties she had on. His smile grew as she sat up, dragging his shirt up his chest. He pulled it the rest of the way off and tossed it on the floor.

Roni leaned in to capture one of his nipples between her lips, closing her teeth over it. Joe knelt, watching as she bit down, and his cock twitched in his jeans. She adjusted herself to kneel in front of him, placing her hands on his chest. "You are pure sin, Joe Blackshaw."

His chuckle came out deep and throaty. "What exactly does that mean?"

Her fingers moved down his chest, slipping into the waistband of his jeans before popping button after button, releasing his cock. "Commando," she whispered on his lips as her hand wrapped around him.

"Fuck." His eyes closed at the sensation. "Always, when I'm not working," he moaned as she stroked him a few times.

"Joe, come for me." Her breath was hot on his lips. "Let it go."

His eyes opened to see hers dancing with an erotic glow he had never seen in a woman. Not that he'd ever really looked, but this woman in front of him held something in his heart. She meant something to him, though he hadn't a clue what it was or what the fuck was happening to him. But he wasn't running. He was going to do what Al told him to do and just let it go, let it happen.

Her mouth touched his, her grip tightened around him, and that was it. He came, and he came hard. Grabbing her head, he deepened the kiss, kissing her deeply. When he finally came down from his orgasm, he bit her bottom lip. Her face was full of light when he pulled back, her green eyes dancing, and that sultry smile nearly did him in.

"Jesus," he whispered as his thumb ran across her bottom lip. "I owe you a release."

She just smiled at him as she moved away. Joe looked down, seeing her stomach and jeans were covered in his release. He got up and grabbed two washcloths, handing her one for her hand, then gently laid her back and proceeded to clean her off.

"Your jeans are a mess." He pulled them off, taking in every inch of her porcelain skin. After tossing them onto the floor, his fingers moved to the sides of her panties. "May I?"

The look on her face stopped him from moving. He wasn't sure what he saw flash in them, but it made him uncomfortable, so he let go and crawled up her body. Resting on his side, he pulled her to him.

"Tell me what I just saw." His voice was gentle.

"Nothing."

"Roni, this is only going to work if you talk to me. I can't assume what is in your head." He could see she was uncomfortable lying there naked, so he sat up and grabbed the blanket at the end of the bed and covered her. He watched as she grabbed at the blanket, and reached down to gently touch her face. "Talk to me."

Taking a deep breath, she said, "Before, it was sort of revenge. I guess I'm a bit nervous now."

He smiled. "That's fine. We will do this at your pace. I'm not going anywhere. You've been in my head for months. I'm crossing a line here, but I know I want you. I want whatever you want to give me."

"What if it's everything I want to give you?"

Leaning in, he sweetly kissed her. "Then give me everything."

"What will I get? Because I don't want to give you everything if you are going to walk away again."

"I didn't walk away last time. You did, and please believe me when I say this to you. I'm not going anywhere. I am not going to take what you give me and not give it back."

"What if I fall in love with you?"

"I'm good with that because I really think I'm falling in love with you." He pulled her to his chest. "Come on, let's get some sleep. We have all the time in the world."

He felt her relax against him. Kissing her forehead, he closed his eyes.

"Why are you being careful with me now?"

He chuckled as his fingers moved up and down her arm. "I was just coming off a huge case. I had made the decision to quit, and I wasn't handling it very well. There was a great deal of pent up energy, anger, adrenaline, and well, I'm an asshole. I needed, no wanted, to get laid."

"Gee, thanks."

Joe laughed and pulled her on top of him, wrapping her in his arms. "You pissed me off when you came over here all dressed up like some kind of slut. I'm not a man who deals well with high maintenance princesses who think they deserve the world. When I decided I didn't care, and then I saw you stripped down, no makeup, being yourself, you fucking blew me away." His hands trailed up and down her back to her ass. "And this ass," he cupped it, "what an incredible ass. I was just being an asshole."

"And now, why so sweet now?"

"Because something inside of me changed. When I saw him dragging you out of that restaurant, with a gun in his hand, something changed. I was so scared, and I don't get scared. Not doing what I used to do. Fear was never an option, but I was afraid."

"Of what?"

"Of never getting to touch you again. Of never getting to taste you again. You taste so sweet. I was afraid he was going to hurt you, and I don't think I would have recovered from that. I was more afraid of losing you in that moment than I was watching that fucker shoot my brother."

Roni picked her head up to look at him. "When I saw you standing there, I wasn't afraid anymore."

Joe rolled over, pushing his hand in her hair. "No?"

She shook her head. "No," she whispered.

"I'm sorry for being an asshole and treating you like a whore. That will never happen again."

"No?"

"No, sweetheart." He kissed her, pulling her into his cocoon. "Let's get some sleep."

"You still have your jeans on," she purred into his neck.

"I do."

He felt her smile. "You can take them off if you want."

"Yeah? Because I really want to."

"It's fine." She giggled.

"You might not think that way in the morning."

"Take them off, Joe."

Rolling onto his back, he managed to get his jeans off and toss them on the floor before pulling her back into his cocoon. She was warm against him. He couldn't remember the last time he'd held a woman like this, and damn if she didn't feel right. "Go to sleep, Roni. I'm not going to ravish you tonight."

"Mmm, what if I wanted you to?"

"Not yet, sweetheart. Not yet."

Joe's whole body shivered when she sleepily giggled into his chest. "Why not yet?" Her arm snaked around his neck as she pressed herself closer.

"Goodnight, Roni."

"Goodnight, Joe."

Not ever knowing when she was going to get pulled out of bed and beaten, Roni turned into a light sleeper. She had heard a thump and sat up, her heart racing when she realized she wasn't at home, nor was she alone. She panicked, moving off the bed.

She watched as the man in the bed sat up next to her. "What's wrong?" Frozen, unable to move, she just stood there. She watched him move, and then the light came on. "Roni, what's wrong?"

Her breaths were coming in short puffs of panic, her eyes darting around the room then back to Joe as he moved to stand. Before she could run, he was pulling her to him, wrapping her in his warmth. The thump happened again, only this time she felt the vibration in the floor. Pulling away from Joe, she looked at him. "He's here. He's coming," she whispered, looking around for a place to hide.

"Who's here? Who's coming?"

There was a thump again, and she turned toward the door. "Tony."

"Hey." Joe turned her to face him. "He is not coming. He's in jail. He doesn't know where you are. Roni, I won't let him hurt you."

She went willingly into his embrace. For some reason, she trusted him. She felt safe with him, but she was naked. She needed some clothes on, just in case. Pulling out of his embrace, she moved to the closet. Joe grabbed his jeans and was sitting on the bed when she came out dressed.

Looking at him, her heart lurched. He was so fucking beautiful, so powerful, so dangerous. He would keep her safe. When she walked over to him, he pulled her into his arms and onto his lap. "I won't let him hurt you." His voice was soft. Roni smiled at him, nodding.

Another thump, this time harder. "Do you hear that?"

Joe shook his head. "No, sweetheart, what do you hear?"

"A thumping. I felt the floor vibrate. It's what woke me up."

Joe stood, steadying her on her feet, and grabbed his gun out of the nightstand. As he moved toward the door, Roni stood there freaking out. She moved like a gazelle running for its life to catch up with him. The thud happened again, only this time it was louder. "There, that. Did you hear it?" she whispered.

"I heard it," Joe whispered back.

She wrapped her hand around his arm. "Joe."

He stopped moving. "This place is as secure as Fort Knox. Nothing is getting in here."

Just as he finished speaking, Roni watched in horror at the scene before her. The huge wooden inside door off the deck bowed as if God himself was pushing on it.

"Fuck," Joe yelled. Grabbing her hand, he took off into the bedroom, shoving her into the closet. "Stay there," he told her, just as the door came crashing in. It sounded like a cannon going off. Joe had just grabbed the phone and was at the closet door when she heard the bear.

She couldn't stop the scream as it came barreling in the bedroom right as Joe slammed his hand on a red button on the wall of the closet. A steel door came slamming down, nearly cutting the bear's paw off.

Roni fell to the floor screaming, pushing herself to the back wall. Joe dropped his gun and his phone and went after her, pulling her into his arms. "It's all right. We are safe in here. It's a safe room. He's not getting in here."

She was hyperventilating, couldn't catch her breath. She finally passed out.

~

"Fuck!" He felt for a pulse. She was still alive and breathing, so he laid her down and grabbed his phone to dial the sheriff. "Hey, Steve, it's Joe Blackshaw."

"Oh, hey, Joe, it's been a while. What can I do for you?"

"Yeah, I'm up at the cabin, and it seems I've got a pretty big bear in my house."

"Don't you have security doors?"

"I do, and he came through them. I had a run in with him just after dark last night. He left, so I locked the place up. Apparently, he is back with a vengeance. Listen, I'm locked in the safe room, and he is beating on the door. Do you think you can get the ranger out here?" Joe flipped on the cameras. "Yeah, he's pissed. I can see him on the cameras. Looks like he's hurt. There's blood everywhere."

"If he got through those doors, I bet he is hurt. All right, you stay put. I'll call out there, and we'll be out shortly. You stay in that room."

Joe chuckled. "I'm not going anywhere."

He disconnected the call and moved back to Roni, picking her up and holding her in his arms. He sat there looking at her. She was so beautiful. His fingers trailed along her jaw, his thumb across her cheek. "Beautiful," he whispered.

Her eyes started to move, then she slowly opened them and looked at him. "I passed out?" Joe nodded. "I do that when things get too hard to handle."

"We are safe. The sheriff and the park ranger are on their way."

"I'm sorry I freaked out like that."

"Don't ever apologize. I can't even begin to imagine what it was like for you. But please know that I would never hurt you like that. I will always protect you."

Her hand reached up to touch his face. "I know."

He couldn't help himself. Lifting her so he could kiss her, he gently licked her lip and she opened up to him. Swipe after swipe, his tongue danced with hers. Before he realized it, they were lying on the floor, kissing each other, gently touching, nothing hurried. He wanted her, but not like this. The time was not now.

"God, Joe, I want you."

Chuckling, he rolled over, pulling her on top of him. "Me too, but not here, not like this. But I must say, we will be doing that again."

Roni giggled. "I won't argue. But we have a bigger problem."

"Mmm, what's that?"

"There's a pissed off bear out there that wants to eat us."

Joe turned his head to look at the monitor. "Yeah, he's pretty angry. I should get dressed. The sheriff and the ranger should be here soon."

He helped her up. "What will they do to him?"

"Tranquilize him, move him out of the area. Not sure, but he's hurt.

Roni turned around to look at the monitor. "How do you know he's hurt?"

Joe grabbed a shirt and pulled it on. "You see those marks on the door?" She nodded. "That's blood, and I know it's not ours." Joe pulled her to his chest. "I was so fucking scared when you passed out. Can I ask you something?" She nodded. "When he would hurt you, did you pass out like that?" He felt her body tense. "I don't want to know what he did to you, not unless you want to talk about it, but you don't need to. Just know that you don't. But I need to know what to expect when certain things happen between us. I don't want you passing out and slamming your head into something."

Roni leaned into him. "Yes. When it would get bad, yes. He kept smelling salts all around the apartment, so he could wake me up."

His arms grew a bit tighter around her. "I'm so sorry."

"I don't know why I stayed. But thank you."

"I don't know why my sister stayed either. Her husband murdered her. He beat her to death and none of us knew. We were busy with our own lives, and no one knew. She never said a word."

"She was probably scared. He more than likely threatened all of you. Tony told me that if I told my father, he would ruin his career."

Joe could feel her trembling. "Hey." He turned her around. "I will say it as often as you need to hear it. I will never hurt you like that."

A shy smile crossed her lips. "Will you hurt me like you did the first time?"

Joe couldn't help himself; he busted out laughing. "Oh, sweetheart, you can count on it."

She wrapped her arms around his waist. His eyes moved to the monitors. "The ranger and sheriff are here."

She turned to look. "How are they going to do this? That bear is huge."

Joe let her go and moved to the monitors. "He's not as big as you think he is. He's just very angry. I don't know why. I've never seen or heard of a bear doing something like this. They will have to lure him outside, then once they tranquilize him, he is going to be pissed and there is no way to outrun him." They stood there and watched. The bear turned his head toward the bedroom door. "They got his attention." Joe watched as the bear moved through the door and disappeared from the room. His eyes moved to the next screen, finding the bear was in the living room.

"Do you think we can go out now?"

"No, not until he is down."

The next monitor showed the bear outside the cabin, where the ranger shot him. It took a few minutes before he slowly lay down. Joe hit the red button, and the door opened. Taking Roni's hand and his gun, they made their way out into the living room.

"Jesus," Roni whispered when she saw the damage. "Look at all the blood."

Joe's eyes were locked on the bear out on the lawn. The sheriff came walking up and they shook hands. "Steve, I've never seen anything like this," Joe said.

The sheriff turned to look at the bear. "Me neither. But you aren't the first one to have a problem with this guy. He's been running around up here all summer long. He's just never gone after someone before. Must be that aftershave you wear." He laughed.

"Yeah."

The ranger walked up. "Looks like this boy has rabies, which would explain the aggressive behavior. We are going to have to put him down."

"Where would he get rabies from?" Joe was concerned. "If one has it, then is it fair to assume others do as well?"

"Yes, it is. Listen, it might not be a good idea for you to stay out here this winter. It's going to take a great effort to find them, to track this one's movements."

Joe looked at the sheriff. "Steve, know any places in town for rent?"

Steve laughed. "I know that you, my friend, don't do town. Don't you have another place where you can camp out for the winter?"

Joe laughed. "I suppose you're right. Yeah, I do. Do you know what Johnny's up to today? I'm going to need these doors fixed."

"Not sure, give him a call. You'll probably want to go sooner rather than later. I need to help these guys. Good to see you." Steve shook his hand and nodded to Roni, then walked away.

Joe pulled his phone out and made a call. Roni started to clean up. When he finished his call, he headed back inside to help her.

"So, you're leaving?" she snapped at him.

Chuckling, he walked over to her. It was when she cowered that he stopped moving. "I know it's a reaction, but please don't ever do that again. I will never hurt you like that. Ever. I'm not leaving. We are leaving. Together. I'm not leaving you here. Not now."

The storm raging in her eyes brewed with darkness he wasn't sure he'd ever seen before. "I have a perfectly good house. I'm not leaving. I just got a job."

"Your house is not safe. Not now, and you know it. You don't need a job, not right now."

She tilted her head. "You don't own me. I may not need a job, but I want one. I want a life. I want to feel like I have some kind of life. You don't know what he took from me!" she shouted.

"No, I don't, but I'd like to know. I'd like to know everything there is to know about you. Roni, it's not safe to stay here right now. We have a house in the Caribbean I'd like to take you to. Will you go with me?"

Shaking her head, she continued to clean up. Joe helped, neither of them saying anything. He wasn't sure what was going on in her head, but with the way she was moving and slamming things around, he was pretty sure she was pissed off. He was being a possessive asshole, and he knew it. But she wasn't safe here.

As they finished, she said, "What do you mean by not now?"

Joe stood there looking at her. "Come here," he said softly. She shook her head. "Roni, come here." He smiled at her.

"Tell me. This isn't going to work if you don't talk to me, Joe."

He laughed, stepping toward her. She stepped back a step. They moved like this until she was against the wall. Joe smiled as he closed in, his hand wrapping around her neck. "Not now that I've tasted you. Not now that I know what you feel like against my skin. Not now that you want to give me everything. Not now, Roni. Not now. Let me take you away from here."

She swallowed. "All that?"

"Yes, all that, and more if you want it."

Her eyes betrayed her. Joe had never bothered to look at a woman like this. But this woman was becoming everything to him. He was excited to learn all there was to know about her. She was becoming all he ever thought or dreamed that he wanted in life. The lines he was crossing were becoming a blur in his reality. A blur to everything, because she was becoming everything.

Standing there looking at one another, he watched as the storm settled in her eyes and the fire changed to something else. Something he felt pull at his heart. "I'm not sure I can do this. I'm not sure."

His thumb swiped across her lips. "I don't think I've ever been surer of anything in my life. Come with me, Roni. Come with me and let me love you."

His smile was automatic when her eyes changed yet again. He was going to enjoy knowing this woman.

"Love? Let you love me?" She pushed on his chest.

Joe stepped back, chuckling. "Yes!" he shouted, causing her to jump and cower away. "Yes, damn it. Love you. Because I don't know what else this is, this feeling of desperation to keep you close to me, to keep you safe. To devour you, to taste every inch of you. To fight with you, to make up with you."

She stood there looking at him. "Possess me?"

"Every fucking inch of you."

"Don't I get a say in what I want?" Her tone was hurtful, her words cutting him.

Joe stepped aside. "Nothing is stopping you from leaving. Go!" he shouted. "Just fucking go." He was quick to move around her. He didn't want to startle her any more than she already was. Walking into the bedroom, he slammed the door.

He had no clue how to have a relationship like this, how to give and take. He was being an asshole and he knew it. But now he was just pissed off at himself for acting like a child.

Roni stood there watching him. She was nearly positive he was going to grab her, hurt her. But he just walked away. It was the slamming of the door that triggered her tears. She felt this man to her core, and that scared the shit out of her. She wasn't sure what was happening to her. Never had she felt a fraction of this with Tony. Even when he took her virginity, he wasn't that gentle with her. He never touched her like Joe did, and he certainly never looked at her like Joe did.

Slowly, she turned to look at the bedroom door. She could hear him slamming things around in there, positive he was packing his things. Did she want to be left alone? Shaking her head, she answered herself. For the past few months, all she could do was think about this man. Her feet moved her across the room. When she opened the door, there was a suitcase on the bed.

When he stormed out of the closet with his hands full of clothes, he stopped when he saw her. She slowly shook her head.

"I'm so scared." Her words were a whisper.

He dropped what he was holding and was across the room, wrapping her into his arms. "So am I. For different reasons, but so am I."

Roni wrapped her arms around his shoulders, pushing on them. Joe lifted her, and she wrapped her legs around his waist, as he pressed her into the wall next to the door. "So afraid, Joe."

Joe wiped her tears. "I know, sweetheart. I know."

She had to tell him how she felt. Keeping it locked inside of her was what kept her a prisoner with Tony. Taking a deep breath, she let it all out. "I think I'm in love with you, and I'm so afraid that I'm going to lose me. I am just finding who I am again."

"Aww, beautiful, I don't want you to lose yourself. I want you to be free of the torment, free of the prison he kept you in, and I'm not stupid to think I can do that for you. But I want to help you. I want to love you. Will you let me?"

"Do you love me, Joe?" Her whisper was nearly soundless.

"I don't know what love is, but I'm willing to find out. I just know how I feel right now, how I've felt since that first day." His lips nearly touched hers, his eyes boring into her.

She swallowed. "How do you feel right now?"

"Like I can't breathe."

She moved her head that last inch and touched his lips with hers. What she experienced when he took control of the kiss warmed her from her toes to her head. The passion she felt was something she couldn't ignore. She would be a fool to think this was just a fun time. He felt for her; she knew it now.

"Yes, I'll go with you. Yes." Her tears just came. She couldn't explain why she was crying. Maybe it was fear, maybe it was happiness, or maybe she just needed to know that life and love were something more than torment and fear.

CHAPTER SEVEN

Joe stood there holding this incredible creature in his arms. He didn't understand why her tears were falling. Hell, he didn't understand a fucking thing about women. He just knew that when she was in his arms, nothing else mattered to him but her. Not the fact that she was his friend's daughter or the fact that she was coming off a year of some serious abuse. He just knew how he felt, and that was complete.

To him, she was the part of him that was missing. Not understanding any of it, he just smiled at her and wiped her tears. Her eyes mesmerized him. The myriad of emotions that moved through them baffled him. But he had not one doubt that he wanted to spend a lifetime looking into them and learning what each look meant.

The slamming of a car door snapped him out of his trance, bringing him back to the here and now. "Someone's here." His voice carried nothing but desire for her. She nodded, and he felt her legs release from his hips. "No," he whispered on her lips, kissing her, making her feel everything he was feeling, if that were possible.

Pulling back, he pulled her lip between his teeth. Her smile was the one thing he wanted to see. "Someone's knocking on the door," she whispered as her fingers touched his lips. "Joe Blackshaw, please be careful with me. I really think I might be in love with you."

"I will never hurt you." Joe smiled at her, wiggling his eyebrows. He smacked her on the ass, causing her to yelp.

Joe let her go, adjusted his cock, and headed to the door. It was Johnny, the man who made the security doors for him.

"I heard you had a rabid bear up here," he said as he came in.

"Yeah, and he did a number on the doors. Listen, I'm going to need you to give them a quick fix and then make me something a bit more solid or a way to reinforce these. I'm headed out of here for the winter. Ranger said there could be more bears with rabies, and I'm not so sure I want to deal with them."

"Not a problem. He didn't take them off the hinges, so I should be able to lock them up for you until spring, when you get back."

"Thanks. How long do you think it will take?"

"A few minutes."

"Thanks," Joe said as he watched him work.

Ten minutes later, Johnny told him, "That should hold you until I can get a new set for you."

"Thanks, John. We'll see you when I get back."

"Not a problem. You have a great holiday. Happy Thanksgiving."

"You too. Tell Judy I send my best."

"Will do."

When Johnny left, Joe headed back to the bedroom where he found Roni lying on the bed. Crawling up her body, he paused and gently bit her ass. Pulling her to him, he touched her face. "You ready to go?"

"Are you sure you want to do this?"

He kissed her. "So very sure. Do we need to stop off and pick up some of your clothes?"

"Probably. I don't want to take my father's plane. I don't want him to know where I am."

"I really should go talk to him."

"No, you really shouldn't. Can't we just have this for us right now? I think there's been enough drama. I would like to just be normal for a while."

"Normal it is." Joe rolled them off the bed. Taking her hand and grabbing the bags, they left his cabin and drove to hers.

While she was packing her bag, he called Jason. "Hey, man, I'm going to need the plane. My cabin had a run in with a rabid bear. The place is trashed. The ranger suggested I stay away for a while until they can track the movements and make sure there aren't anymore."

"Holy shit. You all right?"

"Yeah, I'm fine. Barely made it into the safe room, but all is good. I'm going to head down to the house in the Caribbean for the winter. You good with that?"

"No problem. I'll send the plane. Listen, Mike called to hire us again. Apparently, the judge wants Veronica in the courtroom. This asshole has a hell of a lawyer, and the judge thinks he might just get off."

"No fucking way. The bastard shot you. How can he get off?"

"His lawyer is playing it off as self-defense. Says I threatened him."

"Jason, have you spoke to the DA?"

"Yeah, he said it's not up to him anymore."

"Send the damn plane. I'll be back. There is no fucking way that asshole is getting off."

"All right, I see you when you get here."

Joe hung up and looked at the stairs. She should have been down already. He was moving, taking two stairs at a time. When he walked into Roni's bedroom, she was sitting on the bed with her phone in her hands having a complete meltdown.

Joe got on his knees in front of her. "Hey."

Her eyes moved to his. He could see nothing but fear in them. "I have to go back."

Joe wanted to pull her into his arms, but he didn't want to freak her out. "I know, I just talked to Jason. I'm going with you. I won't let him hurt you."

"You can't go with me. We can't tell my father about us. Not yet."

"I know, but I will be the one protecting you, not Jason or Ben. Me."

Her hand came up and touched his face. "I'm so scared, Joe. He could get away with this."

"If he does, and if he comes after you, I'll be there. I won't let him hurt you."

She nodded. "My dad sent his plane for me. We need to go."

Joe nodded as he stood, pulling her into his arms. "Let's go. I have to wait for my plane, but he is still in jail so you'll be safe. I will pick you up to go to court."

She nodded into his chest. "I don't want to leave you."

"I don't want you to go," he whispered against her head.

They separated, and Joe grabbed her bag. Together they headed to the airport. When they pulled up, Roni asked, "Can I have your phone?" Joe handed her his phone, and she dialed her number. "Now, I have yours and you have mine."

Joe grabbed her and pulled her onto his lap, kissing her hard. "I'm right here." He put his hand on her chest, over her heart. "I'm not going anywhere. Believe that."

"I believe you. Please don't hurt me, Joe Blackshaw."

"I will never hurt you. I really believe I'm in love with you."

He watched the tears form in her eyes. "Good, because I'm in love with you."

Joe wiped her tears, kissing her again, this time a bit gentler. "Come on, you need to get on that plane. I'm four hours behind you. Go straight to your father's. I'll call you when I land."

Roni nodded, climbing off his lap, and they got out of the car. Joe grabbed her bag and watched her walk to the plane. Then she was gone.

Walking away from him was one of the hardest things she'd ever done. But the drama her father would instill if he knew about them is not something she wanted or needed right now. He was going to go batshit crazy. Joe Blackshaw was his friend. She sat and looked out the window as he drove to the garage. She knew he would go inside and wait for his plane to come. It wasn't right that he had to wait.

Standing, she walked up to the pilot. "Tanner, can you hold on a minute? We are going to have one more passenger. I'll be right back."

"Yes, Miss Holloway."

Roni climbed down the stairs and took off running across the tarmac to the private waiting area. When she burst through the doors, Joe turned to look at her.

"It's ridiculous that you have to wait four hours for a plane when I have a perfectly good one right there. We are going to the same place, so just come with me."

His smile was plastered across his face. Roni didn't think she had ever seen a smile like that. He was stunning.

"Well, who am I to turn down a beautiful woman?" Turning, he asked the man at the desk to notify his pilot to turn around. He told him it wouldn't be a problem. Joe grabbed his bag, and they headed out to her plane.

"You do know that there will be questions about this," he said softly.

"I decided I don't care. Do you care, Joe?"

"I care because he is my friend. But other than that, nope, don't care."

Roni started to giggle. "I think, as long as we remain professional, no one will be the wiser."

"Oh, woman, you are asking a great deal of me. How am I supposed to remain professional when all I want to do is lay naked in bed with you for days at a time?"

Roni smiled. "In due time, Mr. Blackshaw. In due time."

They boarded the plane, and the flight attendant took Joe's suitcase and stored it away. Ten minutes later, they were flying down the runway headed back to L.A., back to face her demons. Back to face the man who had tortured her. Looking at Joe, finding his eyes watching her, she gave him a small smile. He nodded.

They didn't talk on the flight. They didn't even sit by one another. Roni was trying with all that she was to muster up her courage. In less than twelve hours, she had to face Tony in court. She had to tell the jury what he had said to her, what he was planning to do to her, and Joe would be sitting there listening. She wasn't sure she could do it.

When she looked at him, he nodded to her. His eyes watched her like a hawk watching its prey. It was unnerving but comforting at the same time. Twisting her hands, she looked out the window; L.A. was down below. Her nerves were getting the better of her. Now, she had so much to live for. She had Joe, and he wanted her just as much as she wanted him.

The pilot came on and said they were starting their descent. Fifteen minutes later, they were taxiing to the private hanger. She knew her father would have a car waiting for her, but should she ask Joe if he wanted a ride? Closing her eyes, she tried to remain calm, but there was no way that was going to happen.

The plane stopped, and the pilot opened the door. Roni just sat there. She wasn't sure she could walk. Joe didn't move; he was waiting for her. Taking a deep breath, she stood, grabbed her bag, and walked off the plane to the waiting car. As the driver shut her door, she looked out the window at the plane, where she saw Joe still sitting in his seat looking at her. She put her hand on the window as they drove away.

Joe closed his eyes and took a deep breath before standing and walking off the plane. Jason had a truck parked in the private lot for him. Struggling with himself not to go to the Senator's house, he headed to the office. When he walked in, the young girl at the desk stood.

"Mr. Blackshaw, your brothers are waiting for you."

"Thank you." He headed to Jason's office. When he opened the door, he was shocked to see Al and Becca sitting there.

Becca was the first to her feet, stepping into his embrace. "We've been so worried about you," she said softly as Joe hugged her. "You are staying with us. We need to talk." Her whisper was so soft, it was heard only by him.

Joe chuckled. "Hi to you, too."

Becca pulled back, smacking him on the chest. Al was right behind her, grabbing his brother in a hug.

Jason and Ben sat there smiling. It had been a long time since they were all together like this. Joe sat down. "So, tell me what the fuck is going on?"

Jason began. "Well, this fucker has a hell of a lawyer. I did hit Eden, at Mike's place, but I was defending Veronica. I did threaten him, so he does have a valid point of self-defense. He says he felt threatened by my presence." Jason laughed. "The fucker shot me. I was just standing there."

Joe could feel Al's eyes on him as his anger built. "What about Holloway's daughter?"

"The judge thought it was best if the jury heard her testimony instead of just reading the transcript. I personally think his lawyer is going to twist her words, make her look like she is crazy. Mike said Eden tried to convince him that Veronica had a mental problem, so I think they are going to move on that."

"Where is Mike?"

"As far as I know, he's at his house. Veronica is supposed to be coming back. She has to be in court in the morning. I've got eight guys at his house. Ben and I are going to escort her to court."

Joe shook his head. "I'll be escorting her." Turning, he looked at Al. "I need to head to Mike's. You going to be at your place?"

Al looked at Becca. "I'll go with you, and yes, we are staying at the loft."

Joe's eyes shifted to Becca's. She smiled at him. "Well then, let's go. I need to eat and then sleep for a bit." He looked at Jason. "This is fucking bullshit, and I promise you, brother, he isn't getting out."

Jason watched Joe, nodding to him. Al and Joe left and headed to Mike's house.

In the car, Al didn't waste any time. "So, tell me, brother."

"I am so fucked, Al. I seriously think I'm in love with this girl. She is the sweetest thing I've ever tasted."

"Jesus, I don't want the intimate details." Al laughed.

"Wasn't going to give you any. I am so freaked out by what is going on right now. This fucker tormented her. On the plane, she didn't say a word. I just sat there and watched her try to get control."

"Does Mike know?"

"No, but I'm sure, after this, he is going to have an idea. But you know what? I don't care. He knows I am a man of stature, and he knows I will take care of her."

Al put his hand on his shoulder, giving it a gentle squeeze. "You are, indeed. I can't wait to meet her."

"Hey, why are you here anyway?"

"Becca insisted. She said it was about time you found someone to love, and when she heard this fucker might get off, she made me come. She just wants you to be happy."

"Well, I'll have to thank her for that. She does make me happy. God, when she gets angry, I can barely control myself. The expressions in her eyes are like watching the sky as it changes colors."

Al busted out laughing. "Man, you've got it bad."

Joe laughed. "I do."

When they pulled up to Mike's house, they passed through the gate. As they walked up to the door, Mike opened it and greeted them both. "Come on in. I'm so glad you are going to be taking over. No offense, but I would rather have the two of you."

Al chuckled. "I'm only here because my wife insisted. This fucker shot my little brother. If anything else, he is going down for that."

"Well, Veronica came home this morning. She is up in her room, terrified. Elizabeth isn't being much help. She started in on her the minute she walked in the door."

Joe was pissed. "Mike, what time does Veronica need to be in court?"

"Nine."

"All right, we have eight guys outside. Al and I will be here in the morning to escort you to the courthouse. The press is going to go batshit crazy with this. I saw the trucks outside starting to set up already. This is going to be a nightmare. Maybe it would be a good idea to get her out of here tonight. Al's place, as well as Jason's, is basically unknown."

"I can pull the truck into the garage, and they won't see her getting in. She has got to be a mess," Al offered.

Mike gave a nervous chuckle. "I'm terrified for her. She was crying when she came in. Let me send the maid up to get her. I think that might be the best solution. At least she won't be alone. When she is here, she just stays in her room. I'll be right back."

They watched Mike leave the room, and Al turned to Joe. "Is this the best idea?"

"I can't leave her alone. You didn't see her on that plane. I can't even imagine what she is feeling," Joe said softly.

Mike came back into the room. "She'll be down in a few minutes. Can I get you guys something to drink?"

"No, thank you. I'm going to go pull the truck in the garage," Al said.

"I'll go with you, show you where to go." Mike walked with him out of the room.

Joe stood with his back to the doorway, his heart slamming in his chest. He was hoping he could keep his emotions in check and be professional when he saw her. He felt a hand on his back, startling him, and spun around to find Elizabeth Holloway standing too close to him. Stepping back, he said, "Elizabeth," nodding and stepping back again.

"Joseph, to what do I owe this pleasure? And what a pleasure it is," she purred at him.

This woman had been trying to fuck him for twenty years. But, man, he wanted nothing to do with her. "I'm here to protect your daughter."

"But Mike said you retired. I don't know why she needs protecting. She just needs to get over all of this. Tony is a good man. He will give her a good life. God knows she needs to stop being so dependent on her father for things."

Joe nearly laughed. "Elizabeth, why would you think that a man who beats a woman is a good man?"

"Oh, Tony has assured me that he never beat her. He slapped her a few times, but she deserved it. She has a mouth on her. She needs to learn a bit of respect. Men like when a woman respects them. She has let herself go, gaining all that weight. Veronica just needs to mature. That girl is so immature and spoiled rotten. Michael gives her everything she wants. Look, he dragged you out of retirement because she is playing her poor me card. I swear she has some serious mental problems. Maybe Tony is right. Maybe we should consider getting her in a treatment facility."

She stepped closer to him. Joe backed up, moving around the couch. "Why would you say something like that about your own daughter?"

Elizabeth laughed. "She is thirty years old. She thought going to college would make her an acceptable catch. She wants to be a grade school teacher. Who aspires to be that? She was raised to be the wife of a man with prestige, not a school teacher." As she spoke, she moved toward Joe. "Joseph, we are two lonely people. Michael is away a great deal, and he is growing older. I know you don't have anyone in your life. What would you think about the two of us getting together?"

Joe chuckled. "Elizabeth, I will tell you the same thing I've been telling you for the past twenty years. It will never happen."

Roni was standing in the hallway listening to her mother. When she came downstairs, she heard Joe's voice and her heart stopped. But as she listened to her mother throwing herself at him, she became angry.

Stepping into the doorway, she watched her mother move on Joe. A smile crossed her lips as Joe constantly moved away from her. When she heard Joe say nothing would ever happen between them, she cleared her throat.

Joe turned his head to look at her, and she could see the fear in his eyes. But her smile didn't leave her face.

"Mother, where is Daddy? He sent for me. Who is this?" She nodded to Joe.

Elizabeth stood there shooting daggers at her. "He's your father's friend. You can go back to your room; your father isn't here," she snarled at her. Roni watched her mother turn her attention back to Joe.

"Joseph, let's have a drink."

"Elizabeth, I'm working, and I don't drink when I'm working."

"Working? Michael told me you retired. I still don't understand why you would come out of retirement."

"Well, I did, and I'm here to protect Veronica."

"Then you can have a drink with me. We can get reacquainted. It's been far too long. Veronica doesn't need your attention. Your brothers can protect her."

"Ah, Veronica," Mike said as he walked into the room. "I want you to meet Joe Blackshaw. I'm not sure you two met properly when he drove you home. This is his brother, Al. They have both come out of retirement to protect you until this mess with Tony is finished."

She just stood there looking at her mother. "Michael, is it necessary to hire these men? They are very expensive. Tony just wants to love our daughter." Her eyes stayed on Joe. "I'm sure Joseph has other things to do rather than babysit."

"Elizabeth," Joe started. "He was dragging her out of a restaurant with a gun in his hand. He doesn't love her. He was going to hurt her. I know because I was there."

"Nonsense, your brother beat him up in the front hall. Of course, he had a gun." Her eyes shifted to Roni. "You need to say you're sorry and go back to the man. He is a good match for you and your wild behavior. You need to just be a dutiful wife, maybe have some kids. That should make him happy. It made your father happy."

"Mother, I'm not ever going back. He hurt me. I'm going to court tomorrow, and I'm going to do everything I can to make sure he goes to jail." Turning, she looked at her father. "Daddy, I don't need to be protected. Tony can't hurt me anymore. When this is over, I'm leaving and I'm not coming back."

Her father put his hands on her shoulders. "Sweetheart, you are my only daughter. Joe Blackshaw is the best. He is good at what he does. You are going to go with these men, and they are going to keep you safe. The press is going to be all over this house by morning. They've already started camping outside the gate."

"You want me to go with two men I don't know?" She needed to play it up. Her parents couldn't know about her and Joe, especially not her mother.

Pulling her into his embrace, her father hugged her. "I've known Joe for twenty years. He is an honorable man and will keep you safe. Now, go up and pack a bag. I will be in court tomorrow with you. So, go on now and meet us in the kitchen. We pulled Al's truck into the garage."

She smiled at him. "If you think it's best." Turning, she looked at Joe and Al. "Please excuse me. I'll be down in a few minutes."

Joe nodded to her. Al just stood there with a smile on his face. He knew what was going on. He knew this woman was who his brother was falling in love with. He knew he was looking at his future sister-in-law.

Mike turned to look at Joe. "She isn't in a good place right now. She's terrified." His voice was strained.

"We'll keep her safe," Al promised.

Joe didn't say anything. He was afraid Mike would hear in his words what he was feeling for his daughter.

"It shouldn't take her long. She just got back, so I'm sure her bag is still packed."

Joe looked at Elizabeth and nodded. "Elizabeth, we'll see you in court."

"No, you won't. I am not going to watch her say horrible things about such a good man. She needs to get over this and marry him like we planned."

Joe knew this woman was a bitch, but who the hell talks about their child like that? He went to say something, but Al stopped him.

"Excuse me, Mrs. Holloway, but that good man beat your daughter and shot my brother."

She laughed. "Your brother attacked him in the front hall of this house. I'm sure Tony was afraid your brut of a brother was going to hurt him again. It was self-defense."

Joe chuckled. "You keep believing that, Elizabeth."

She looked at him like she wanted to kill him. "Tony is a good man," she snapped.

Joe saw it in her eyes and shook his head. She'd slept with Tony. This bitch of a woman had sex with her daughter's future husband. Turning, he looked at Mike. Did he know? He was never the kind of man who let his temper get the best of him, and right now, he was struggling to hold on to it. Deciding it was better to walk away, he walked out of the room and headed to the kitchen. Al and Mike followed. Roni was sitting on a stool at the breakfast bar with her bag on the floor next to her.

Joe picked up the bag and walked out the back door. He stood on the porch waiting for Al and Roni, trying to rein in his anger. The door opened, and Al, Roni, and Mike walked out. Joe turned and headed to the garage, not saying a word. He wanted to punch something. Opening the back door, he put her bag in and stood there waiting for her to say goodbye to her father.

As she climbed in, he said softly, "We need you to lay down so the press doesn't see you."

Pausing, she looked at him. Joe could see the confusion in her eyes. A small, gentle smile crossed his lips as he nodded. Roni lay across the back seat, and Joe shut the door.

"Please keep her safe," Mike said to him.

"With my life," Joe said, shaking his hand. He opened the front door and got in, Al next to him.

Pulling out of the gate, Al looked at him. "Care to elaborate?"

"I have no idea what you're talking about."

Al laughed. "Oh, brother, you most certainly do."

"It'll keep."

"Can I sit up, or do I have to lay down all the way there?" Roni smarted.

Al laughed. "You can sit up now."

Joe didn't say a word. He just looked out the window. Pulling up to Al's loft, he jumped out and opened the back door, helping Roni out then grabbing her bag. Al came around, and they put her between them as they walked up to the loft.

Becca was waiting with their dog and cat. She had cooked some food for them. "Hi, I'm Becca, Al's wife," she said to Roni as she hugged Joe. "You all right?" she asked Joe.

"I'm fine. This is Roni."

Roni smiled at her. "Nice to meet you."

Joe didn't look at Roni when he said, "Come on, I'll show you where you're sleeping." He walked into the loft.

Roni just stood there looking at his back, then at Becca, then at Al. Joe kept walking, thinking she was following him. When he got to her room, he turned to talk to her but she wasn't there. He set her bag on the floor and went back into the living room. She was just standing there looking at him. He could see the fire in her eyes, and his heart smiled.

"Are you coming?"

Her eyes became slits, the anger brewing. "I wasn't aware that you were the boss of me. I'm not sure I'm comfortable with being bossed around. What is your problem?" she snapped at him.

Becca laughed. "I made some dinner. Whenever you want to eat," she said to Roni, then to Al, "Why don't you come with me?" She put her hand out.

Al took it, and as they walked by Joe, he slapped him on the shoulder. "Good luck, brother."

"I don't have a problem," he said to Roni.

She folded her arms across her chest. "Try again, Mr. Blackshaw."

Joe stepped forward, and Roni stepped back. He smiled a soft smile. "I'm not playing here."

"This isn't going to work if you don't talk to me."

"Don't throw my words at me." He jumped at her. Her eyes changed to fear. "I'm sorry, I didn't mean to scare you."

She shook her head. "Stop. Just forget it. I don't want to do this with you." She moved around him. "Where is my room?"

"Down the hall, second door on the left. Your bag is next to the bed." He wanted to reach out and pull her to him, but he'd scared her. His anger brewed just below the surface. He needed to get control.

Roni was shaking. She wanted to scream at him, but he'd scared her. Closing the bedroom door, she slid down to the floor and burst into tears, covering her mouth so no one could hear her sob. So much was going on inside of her. She listened to her mother come on to Joe. She wanted to fuck him. Her heart hurt. She couldn't help but wonder if he fucked her.

"Oh God," she whispered.

Standing, she looked for the bathroom, then went in and closed the door. Sitting on the floor, Roni pulled her legs up, wrapping her arms around them. She felt so alone, so afraid. She wondered what the point to all of this was. She was really struggling to maintain her sanity.

Joe stood there feeling like the biggest asshole on the planet. It wasn't her fault her mother did what she did. It wasn't her fault he felt completely helpless in sharing how he was feeling. "Fuck." He ran his hands through his hair. His feet were moving. She was here with him, and that was all that mattered. He gently knocked on her door, but there was no answer, so he opened the door and looked in. The bathroom door was closed, so he walked in. Closing the door, he turned the lock and sat on the bed facing the bathroom door.

When the door opened and he raised his head to look at her, his heart broke. Her eyes were red, her chest still heaving from crying. Joe stood, picked her up, and climbed onto the bed, sitting her on his thighs. Moving his hands up to her face, he gently kissed her.

"I am so sorry for that. So fucking sorry. Aww, sweetheart, please forgive me." He wanted her so desperately.

Shuddering breaths escaped her chest. "Why didn't you say anything to me?"

"You said you didn't want them to know about us yet. If I had spoken to you or looked at you, they would have known. I can't look at you and hide how I feel."

"How do you feel?" Her fingers brushed his lips.

Joe kissed her, laying her back on the bed. "Like I'm going to die if I can't touch you." He felt himself losing control. He couldn't let this happen, not here. Pulling back, he touched her face. "So fucking sweet."

"I don't want to be here. I want to go away."

"I know, me too. But we have to make sure he pays for what he did to you."

"Are you going to be there, in the courtroom?"

"Do you want me to be there?"

"Yes and no. I don't want you to have to listen to the things he did to me. But, then again, I'm not sure I can do this without you."

Joe touched her face as her eyes filled with tears. "Sweetheart, I want to help you deal with this. I told you, you don't have to tell me. If you don't want me to know, then I'll wait outside. Al, Jason, and Ben will be there. Becca will be there."

"But I don't know them."

He smiled. "Well, come on." He pushed up. "You can get to know them. Becca made dinner, and I don't know about you, but I could eat." His voice deepened. "Although, there is something else I would rather have," he whispered on her lips.

"What would that be?" Roni said as her lips brushed across his.

Joe slowly slid his hand up her blouse, cupping her breast. "This." He kissed her as he squeezed. Moving his hand down her body to cup her ass, he pulled her to him as he pressed his cock into her core. "This." He kissed her again, lifting her thigh over his hip, his fingertips pressing into her core. "This, so much this." He kissed her again.

"Please. Oh God, Joe," she moaned.

Joe rolled over, pulling her with him. "I am not the kind of man who waits for what he wants. But we can't do this here."

"I know, but I need to feel you."

"You will, beautiful. Come on, let's go eat and be normal for a while."

Roni sat up on Joe's cock, her eyes rolling in her head. "Oh my God," she moaned as her hips moved back and forth.

His hands held her hips. "You need to stop that." Moaning, he pushed up to gain more friction. "Fuck, Roni." Sliding down his thighs, she undid his jeans, and before Joe could move, she had her mouth wrapped around him. His back arched off the bed as she based him. "Aww, fuck!" His hands shot up to her head to pull her off him, but she fucking swallowed and he lost his shit. His hips jerked as he came, pouring everything down her throat. He had never come that fast in his life. He couldn't remember the last time he'd had a blow job, but this wasn't a blow job. She literally fucked him with her mouth. One push, one swallow, and he was done.

When she took all that he was, she slowly pulled off him, sitting back on her heels to look at him. He watched her eyes, another look he had never seen in a woman. Joe sat up, his hands wrapping around her head, pulling her to him. Slowly, he kissed her, deeply, sensually. He had never kissed a woman like this, and in his heart, he knew he would never kiss another one. He lay back, and she came with him, moving to their sides. "God, sweetheart, what was that?"

Smiling, she shook her head. "I just wanted…"

"Tell me."

"I just wanted to show you how I feel."

"What was wrong with your words? Words are good."

"Joe, I need to ask you something, and I'm terrified."

"You can tell me anything. You can ask me anything. I will not lie to you."

She nodded, touching his lips. "Joe, did you ever fuck my mother?" Her voice was full of so much pain.

Shaking his head, he answered. "No, sweetheart, no. Not ever."

"I heard the things she said to you. I saw her making a move on you."

Joe smiled. "She's been trying to sleep with me for twenty years. I personally can't stand her. I don't think she has ever been faithful to your father. I'm sorry."

"She's never liked me. I'm sure she has never loved me. I don't have any fond memories of my childhood that include her. I think she is jealous of my relationship with my father."

"I'm sorry, sweetheart." Joe pulled her to his chest. "But I would really like to know what that was."

"I was scared that maybe you had a thing with my mother. I think I wanted you to know I was the better choice."

"Hey, listen to me. I would never be the other man in any relationship. I don't sleep with married women, and trust me when I tell you that you are the better everything. There will be no other woman but you. Not now. Not now, sweetheart."

They lay on the bed kissing for a long time. The knock on the door separated them. "Hey, you guys want to eat?" It was Al.

"Yeah, we'll be right there," Joe yelled out. Touching Roni's face, he whispered, "Come on, beautiful." Letting her go, he rolled off the bed, buttoning his jeans.

Roni got up and straightened her clothes, and they headed out to the dining room.

~

Hours passed while they ate and talked, getting to know one another. Roni helped Becca clean up while Joe and Al went out on the balcony to talk.

"Can I say something?" Becca asked her.

"Sure."

She smiled at her. "I've known Joe for probably twenty years. He and my husband were best friends."

"I thought Al was his brother?"

Becca giggled. "They are, my first husband and my children died in a fire a long time ago."

"Oh my God. I'm so sorry."

"Thank you." Becca looked past her to Joe, who was watching Roni. "I've never seen him with a woman before."

Roni turned to look at Joe. "Why not?"

"He's always been about the job. When you do what they do, a relationship isn't an option. They would be gone for weeks at a time. Having someone you love can be dangerous."

Roni turned to look at her. "How do you know he loves me?"

Becca smiled a warm smile at her. "In the past few months since you two met, he would call Al to talk to him about how he was feeling. Your father is his friend, and he is struggling with that. I'm so happy for him, and for you, too. He is a wonderful man, true at heart. He will love you for the rest of your life. Please don't hurt him. He loved only one time before, a very long time ago, but when she found out what he did for a living, she walked away. He has never let himself feel since."

"I've only ever had Tony, and well, we know what happened there. I'm so afraid to let him in. He is kind of full on. It scares me."

Becca laughed. "That he is. But under that bossy, mean demeanor, he is a kind and caring man. One of the best. I've never seen him like this. I'm glad he found you. It's such a good thing to know he is finally there. Finally in that place to open his heart. Please, Roni, don't hurt him. He might not recover."

Roni stood there looking at her. Joe walked up, touching her arm. "You all right?" he asked, looking from her to Becca.

Roni nodded. "I think I'm a bit tired. We have to be up early." Looking at Becca and Al, she told them, "Thank you for dinner, but I think I'm going to head to bed."

Everyone said goodnight and Roni went to her room.

Joe stood there looking at Becca. "What happened?"

Becca smiled at him. "Nothing, just having some girl talk."

"Bec, we've known one another for a long time. That was more than girl talk."

She laughed. "It was, but it's private. You love her, don't you?"

"I'm not sure what it is I feel. I just know that I want to know. I want everything with her."

"Maybe you should tell her that. Joe, she is going through a great deal right now. Imagine how terrified she is to have to face that man. She is going to spill everything in the morning. Tell complete strangers the intimate details of her relationship with him. You know what happened to me. Well, that was nothing compared to what she is dealing with."

"I know, Bec, but I don't know how to help her. How do I get her to let me in?"

Becca smiled at him, putting her hand on his chest. She pushed up on her toes, kissing him on the cheek. "You make her feel safe. That's what your brother did for me. He made me feel safe and warm and so very loved. Do that for her, because she needs it. She feels so alone and scared."

Joe hugged her and then excused himself. He knocked on the bedroom door, but there was no answer, so he opened it. Sticking his head in, he heard the shower, so he went in. He locked the door behind him and sat in the chair to wait for her.

Roni needed to get away from the conversation, so she excused herself. Once in her room, she locked the door, but after thinking about it, she turned the lock. She didn't want Joe to think she didn't want him in there with her. She just wasn't sure she could handle him. Pushing off the door, she stripped out of her clothes then went into the bathroom and took a shower. She stood under the hot water, letting it run over her, and started to cry. In the morning, she'd have to face him. She'd have to tell everything he did to her, and then his lawyer would ask her questions. Questions she wasn't sure she wanted to answer, not with him there. Not with Joe there.

When she walked out of the bathroom, the room was dark. Not turning on the light, she reached for her bag to grab her panties and a t-shirt. When she dropped her towel, she felt him behind her. Then his lips were on her shoulder.

"You are so beautiful." His breath was warm on her skin, his lips soft yet firm.

"I'm so scared. I don't know what I'm doing. What to think, how to act."

"Just be you, sweetheart."

"Are you just being you? Is this the man you are? Or is this an act for my benefit?"

"I'm many faces of the same man. I am this man with you." His hands moved up her arms. "I'm the man I was earlier when I am working. Protecting you is not only my job but my desire as well." His hand moved up her neck, holding her jaw as he turned her head so he could kiss her. "I want to be only this man." His mouth covered hers, his kiss sweet and gentle. "I want to be the man who holds you for the rest of your life. I want to be the only man who has the pleasure of seeing you like this. I want to be the only man." He kissed her again.

"What do you want from me?" Roni whispered as she pulled out of the kiss.

Joe let go of her. Stepping back, he turned around. "Get dressed, Roni." He was angry, but he didn't know why he was angry. He needed to get control. She was feeling very vulnerable, and there was no way he wanted to scare her.

"I'm dressed," she snapped.

Joe turned to look at her. "What is going on in your head? Why would you ask me that?"

"Is this all you want? Sex? Am I to be used by you until you are through with me?"

Joe laughed because, if he didn't, he was going to blow up. "You are an impossible woman."

"Why, because I have a mind? Because I have my own thoughts, come to my own conclusions? You forget, Joe Blackshaw, that I have been manipulated and controlled for a very long time. I wasn't allowed to do anything but listen and learn. You present yourself as a knight in shining armor, but then you are this cold, calculating, hard-core badass. I don't know where I stand or what is expected of me. I am so tired of being manipulated and used. I want my own self back. I want to be me. But I'm not so fucking sure I know who the hell that is."

Joe stood there looking at her. He was sure that if steam could come out of a person's ears, he would look like a steam engine. "Why don't you take your time in finding out who the hell you are and what the fuck it is that you want." Turning, he walked to the door.

"No!" she shouted. "No! You don't get to walk away." She was moving, placing herself between him and the door. "You are not going to just leave."

He leaned in very close to her face. "Isn't that what you want? For me to leave, then come back on my knees? Well, it isn't going to happen. I told you, I don't play games, and I certainly do not have time for a fucking society princess."

The slap shocked the hell out of Roni. She couldn't believe she hit him. "Don't ever fucking call me that again. I am not my mother."

Joe didn't know if he should pick her up and fuck the hell out of her or walk away. "No, you're not your mother, only because I wouldn't fuck her. But if the shoe fits, princess, wear it."

She slammed her hands into his chest, pushing him back, and then slapped him again. "Get the hell out. Get the fuck away from me." She pushed past him and into the bathroom, slamming the door.

"Fuck," Joe sputtered and walked out the door.

When she heard the door slam against the wall, she hurried out. She didn't need this shit, this game playing. "Fuck him," she muttered as she put her jeans and shoes on. Grabbing her bag, she moved through the loft without being noticed. Joe was on the balcony. Al and Becca were nowhere in sight. She walked out the front door and into the night. Not knowing what to do, she just walked. Her phone buzzed a few times in her pocket, but she didn't look at it. In fact, she shut it off without taking it out of her pocket.

"Fuck him. Bastard," she mumbled.

For hours, she wandered the streets. The sky was lighting up, and she knew she had to be in court, but she also needed to shower. Stepping to the street, she put her hand out and hailed a cab. Getting in, she asked to be taken to the Four Seasons.

She checked in and headed to her room. It was six in the morning, so she had three hours before she needed to be in court. She ordered room service and just sat on the bed. Her mind still whirled with emotion, with anger. She was totally devastated by what took place. She shouldn't have hit him. She shouldn't have left, but she wasn't going to be anyone's puppet. She was in love with him, and he was treating her like his possession. She belonged to no one but herself.

The knock on the door brought her back to the here and now. Climbing off the bed, she opened the door and took the tray before thanking the man. As he walked away, she turned to set the tray down, but hands grabbed her and the tray crashed to the floor. Her instincts kicked in, and she slammed her head back, hitting the person behind her in the face.

"Fuck!" he screamed, letting her go.

She spun around, kicking him in the balls and then pushing him out of the way. Opening the door, she took off down the hall to the stairs. When she rounded the corner, she hit a brick wall and fell backward on her ass. Looking up, Al was bending to help her up.

"No!" she yelled. "Don't touch me." Getting to her feet, she saw Joe come out of her room, his face bloody. Her heart lurched in her chest, but she turned and headed for the stairs. By the time she made it to the lobby, Joe was standing outside the doors. He wrapped his arm around her, picking her up, then walked out the side door and put her in an SUV, climbing in next to her.

"Drive," he said as Roni tried to open the other door to get out. Finally, the door opened.

"Oh, no you don't," Joe said as he grabbed her before she fell out of the door. The car was moving, and it was moving fast.

"No, stop." She fought him until the car stopped. Her door opened, and Jason was standing there. He grabbed her, taking her into a building. Joe followed. She fought them every step of the way. Jason walked her into a room and sat her down. She turned to run, but Joe was standing there. Jason walked out and shut the door behind him.

They stood there staring at each other. "Why did you leave?" he barked at her.

"Fuck you!"

"We aren't leaving this room until you talk to me."

"Fuck you. I'm done. I'm going to be late to court. Just leave me the hell alone. I didn't ask for this shit. You don't fucking own me!" she screamed.

Al and Jason stood outside with smiles on their faces. Their brother had his hands full with this woman. She wouldn't take his shit or his moods.

"Veronica..." he started.

"Don't fucking call me that." She moved past him to the door, but Joe grabbed her around the waist, pulling her to his chest.

"Don't run from me," he said calmly.

"I don't want you. I want nothing to do with this. I won't let you control me or my emotions."

"That's not what I'm trying to do." His heart hurt.

"Yes, it is. You just want me so you can have sex. You don't want anything else from me. I'm not going to let you use me like that. Society Princess, remember? I have feelings, emotions, you know?"

"Oh, I know you do. Trust me. Roni, I'm new to this, to this emotional stuff. I don't know what the hell I'm doing. I'm so sorry for making you feel that you needed to run from me. I'm so sorry for saying that to you."

She shook her head. "No, you're not. You're just pissed that I walked out. I don't want this. I can't do it anymore. I'm going to testify against a man who mentally, physically, and emotionally tortured me. I am not about to walk into another relationship with a man who wants to control me. You may not be hitting me to hurt me, but you are fucking hurting me just the same by playing this game with me."

"That's on me then, because I don't know what the fuck I am

doing. You make me crazy. I haven't had anything to do with women and their emotions in a very long time. So, please, let me learn."

"No!" she yelled. "Fucking no! I can't take it. I don't want this roller coaster. I want you to just leave me alone."

Joe let her go. "Let Al and Jason escort you to court, at least, please."

She opened the door and walked out. Al turned to look at his brother and could see the unshed tears in his eyes. Joe nodded to him, and Al walked away, following Roni outside. Ben opened the back door of the SUV, and she climbed in. Al got in the front seat, and Jason drove them back to the hotel. Without stopping, Roni went straight to her room and got in the shower. When she came out, she noticed that the tray had been cleaned up and a fresh one was sitting on the table. Looking at the clock, seeing it was nearly eight, she figured she had just enough time to eat. Then they were on their way to court.

When they arrived, the press was all over the place. Pulling up, they were met by Ben and six other men she didn't know. Al got out and opened her door. The noise was so loud. Al pulled her to his side, and Jason moved to her other side. Ben moved to the front, and two men were behind her. She was cocooned as they escorted her through the throngs of people and cameras. People were shouting at her, some saying horrible things, others asking just as horrible questions.

When they got into the building, she was hyperventilating. "I can't breathe," she whispered. "Al, I can't do this. I can't do this." Her eyes skated across the expanse of the lobby. "I need to use the restroom."

"Roni, we need to get to the courtroom."

"I can't!" she yelled. "I can't do this."

Her father appeared down the hall, walking toward her. "Veronica, come on, we need to hurry."

"Daddy, I can't do this. I can't go in there."

"Sweetheart, the judge cleared the courtroom. It's empty. You can do this. Come on." He wrapped his arm around her waist and started moving down the hall. He was pulling her along. She didn't want to do this.

When they got to the doorway, her father opened the door, ushering her into the courtroom, and sat her at the back of the empty room. Roni sat there trying not to throw up. Her hands shook, and sweat beaded on her forehead. She was trying to get her breathing under control. Al, Jason, and Ben walked in a few minutes after her, and sat down in front of her, blocking her view.

She saw a door open, but she couldn't see who came through it. Then a man said, "All rise for the honorable Judge Simmons." Everyone stood. "Please be seated."

Roni was called to the stand, and the questioning began. She kept her eyes locked on Al, just like he told her to in the car. She refused to look at anyone or anything but Al. An hour later, she was dismissed. Keeping her head down, she made her way back to her seat, where Al escorted her out of the courtroom. She spotted a bathroom across the hall and took off running. She barely made it to the toilet before she threw up.

Her screams just came after each upturning of her stomach. After the third or fourth scream, she felt arms lift her off the floor, wrapping her in warmth as she cried. "Let me take you to Joe. Roni, that man loves you. You need to share this with him. Please let him in," Al said softly. She just nodded. He stood up, carrying her out the door where they were met by Jason, Ben, and two other men.

She kept her head buried in his chest as they made their way back to the car, where Al climbed in the back seat holding her on his lap. Jason made a beeline to the loft, pulling into the garage before the press could find them or see them. Al carried her up to the loft where Joe and Becca were waiting for word from them.

CHAPTER EIGHT

Joe stood and moved like lightning. Al placed Roni in his arms, and he moved into the bedroom, sitting in the chair with her on his lap.

"I'm so sorry, beautiful, so sorry for the things I said to you, the way I treated you," Joe whispered in her hair.

Shaking her head, she cried, "No, I'm the one who is sorry. I didn't mean those things I said. I'm just so scared."

"Shh, I've got you now. God, beautiful."

"Joe."

"Yeah."

"I love you."

"Aww, beautiful, I love you."

Those words warmed her from the inside out. She knew he wouldn't have said them if he didn't mean them. He loved her. She raised her head to look at him. "Really?"

"Oh yeah. You make me crazy. When you walked out that door and left here, I was so scared. I couldn't find you."

"I hurt you. I'm sorry I hurt you." Her hands were on his face, touching his nose and eyes. "Can we leave now? Can we go away? I don't like it here. I want us to be us. I want to know you."

"You have to speak to your father. He called here when Al walked out of the courthouse with you. Then we will go."

"Kiss me, Joe. I need to feel you." Her lips met his.

His hands came up and wrapped around her head, so he could control the kiss. It was deep, long, possessive, and sensual. "So fucking sweet," he whispered. "Come on, beautiful, you need to call your father." He went to stand.

"No. I want to stay here like this with you."

"How about you call your father, and then we can crawl in that bed right there?"

She turned to look at the bed, then back to Joe. "What would we do in that bed?" She was teasing him.

"Anything you would like. I love you, and I don't care who hears me love you."

She felt the heat crawl up her body. She knew he was watching her blush. "I'll get my phone." She moved to get off his lap and he chuckled.

"I'll go out there. Come and get me when you're done."

Roni stopped moving. "No, please stay here. I can't face them, not yet."

Smiling, he nodded as he watched her grab her phone from her bag.

Roni's hands were shaking as she scrolled through her numbers. Finding her father's, she pressed send.

"Veronica, are you all right?"

"Hi, Daddy. I am. I'm sorry about that."

"Where are you? I thought you'd come back to the house."

"Al brought me back to his loft. I'm fine, or I will be fine." She turned to look at Joe, who was sitting there watching her like a hawk. She had to remember to ask him why he did that.

"Are you coming back here?" Her father's voice pulled her from her sinful thoughts.

"I think he wants me to stay here until the press goes away."

"I'll call Joe and talk to him. Why wasn't he there today?"

"He stayed here with Al's wife, just in case the press found this place. Daddy, Joe is right here. Do you want to talk to him?"

"Yes. Veronica, are you sure you're all right?"

"No, daddy. It was so horrible having to relive and say those things. It made me sick just knowing I stayed with him all that time. Do you think he'll get off?"

"I don't know, sweetheart. That was a pretty damning testimony. I was watching the jury. A few of them were wiping tears away, so hopefully, it did the job."

"Okay." Her voice was sad, her body going into shock at the realization that Tony might get off. "Daddy, what if he gets out? He will come for me." Her voice came out barely a whisper.

Joe was out of the chair. He moved to stand behind her so she could feel him.

"Sweetheart, if I have to hire Blackshaw Security to follow you around for the rest of your life, I will. That son of a bitch will never get his hands on you again. Why don't you let me talk to Joe now? Try and get some rest. I love you."

"I love you too, Daddy, and thank you."

Roni turned to look at Joe. She paused for a minute and then handed the phone to him. "My father wants to talk to you."

Smiling, he took the phone from her. "Mike."

"Listen, there is still a chance Tony is going to get off. Can I persuade you to keep an eye on her until this is over? I might have to consider asking you to take this job long term."

Joe chuckled. "I'm retired, Mike. But, yeah, I'll stick around for a few days."

"She's been up at our cabin. I know Tony has no clue it's there, but with Elizabeth on his bandwagon, she may tell him. It's pretty isolated up there. You don't happen to have a place where you can hide her for a while?"

"I think you might be getting ahead of yourself, Mike." Joe's eyes never left Roni's. His hand came up to touch her face. "But I won't let that fucker touch her. And to answer your question, we do have a few places. I'm sure it won't come to that. But Mike, if we have to do this, I can't tell you where she'll be."

"That's fine, as long as she is safe. But keep her there until this is over. The press is insane. It took ten minutes to get through the gate at the house. Your team was instrumental in getting the crowd under control. But they know she isn't here now, and I'm afraid that if he does get out, he'll know she's here and Elizabeth will surely let him in."

"Why would she do that? I don't understand why she wouldn't protect her own daughter."

"I don't know. We've grown apart over the years. There isn't much we talk about anymore. Veronica and Elizabeth's relationship has been strained for years, hell, probably the majority of Veronica's life. I probably should have divorced her years ago, but I didn't want Veronica to have to live alone with her." He released an audible sigh. "You take care of my girl. I'll talk to you in a few days. I need to get back to Washington."

"Hey, Mike, for what it's worth, I'm sorry. Don't worry about her. We'll make sure she is safe. This place is like Fort Knox."

"Thank you, Joe. We'll talk soon."

Joe disconnected the call and handed Roni her phone. They just stood there looking at one another. He watched her eyes; the storm raging in them was mind-blowing. He could see fear, anger, wonder, and then they clouded over, and he saw the desire.

"I'm sorry for making you betray your friend," she whispered, pulling her lip between her teeth.

Joe smiled. "No, you're not." His hand snaked around her waist, pulling her to him.

Roni's hands moved up his chest to his neck. "No, I'm not. Joe, is the door locked?"

"Not sure. Does it matter?" he whispered on her lips.

She smiled. "Yes." He smothered her response with a kiss. Pulling herself up his body, Joe grabbed her thighs and picked her up. She wrapped her legs around him, and he walked them to the door, leaning her against it. His hand moved to lock the door, then he slid them up her sides, taking her blouse with them. They separated so he could pull it over her head. "All of it, Joe. I want all of it, all of you." Her voice was laden with desire.

"You have all of me. I'm very possessive, Roni."

"I know." Her mouth covered his, biting his lip.

"Very demanding."

She giggled. "Oh, I know that."

Joe turned, moving them to the bed. Gently, he laid her down, pulling off her shoes. She undid her slacks and Joe pulled them off. His eyes traveled the length of her. She had on pale pink panties and a bra to match. Reaching behind him, he pulled his shirt off. After kicking off his boots, he undid his jeans, his cock falling out as he dropped them to the floor. "I don't have any condoms." His voice was gruff.

Roni was up on her elbows watching him with her lip tucked between her teeth. "I have an implant," she whispered.

Slowly, he crawled up the bed, kissing her thighs before pressing his lips on her core. As he moved up, his tongue left a trail of goose-flesh along her skin. He pressed his lips to each of her breasts. Looking at her, he whispered, "Turn over, Roni." Her smile told him what he wanted to know. Slowly, she rolled over under him. Pushing up, he looked at her. Sliding his knee between her legs, he unhooked her bra. He put his fingers on the seams of her panties. "I'm sorry about this," he whispered as he tore the lace, slipping the material from under her.

Joe tasted every bit of flesh that he saw. When he reached her ass, he enjoyed it. Biting, licking, sucking the flesh. Her mews drove him to hear more. His hands on her hips, he lifted her perfect ass in the air, sliding his thumb through her core. Bending, his mouth covered her.

"Oh, God," she moaned.

He wanted all of her. Turning her over, he took her slowly in his mouth, watching as her back arched and her hands balled up in the sheet on the bed. She tasted like heaven to him, a beautiful musky taste. When he had his fill, which he didn't believe he would ever get enough of her, he crawled up her body, slowly kissing her.

"I don't want to do this here. When I take you bare for the first time, I want it to be just us," he said softly.

Roni nodded. "Then let's go. I want to go. I don't want to be here anymore." Her fingers touched his face. "Let me up, Joe." Whispering, she kissed him.

"I don't want to. I want to ravish you," he moaned in her mouth.

Giggling, she told him, "The sooner we get out of here, the sooner we can be alone."

Smiling, Joe jumped up off the bed, sending her into a fit of giggles. Turning, he pulled her up and into his arms. "Come, woman. Get dressed and let's get the hell out of here." Giggling, he watched her fish a clean pair of panties out of her bag, grabbing the torn ones off the floor. They got dressed. It didn't matter to him anymore that she was his friend's daughter. He knew he could never be without her. He was going to love this woman until he took his last breath.

When they walked out into the living room hand in hand, Al, Becca, Jason, and Ben were waiting for them. Jason didn't like that they were holding hands, and stood. Looking at Joe, he said in a very hard voice.

"Can I talk to you outside?" He didn't wait for an answer; he just moved to the patio.

Joe looked at Al who had a small smile on his face. "Be careful, our little brother isn't happy with you right now."

After kissing Roni's temple, he walked out on the patio, shutting the door behind him.

"Are you fucking kidding me right now? You're sleeping with her?" Jason snapped.

"To be honest with you, little brother, it isn't any of your business."

"Like fucking hell it isn't. She's the job. You are crossing so many lines here, Joe. You told me not to cross them. Is that the reason? Is that the reason you refused the job, because you are fucking her?"

Joe chuckled. "Be very careful, little brother, how you talk about her."

"You know I wanted her. You did this on purpose."

Joe shook his head. "I had no fucking idea who she was when I turned down the job. I met her long before any of this shit happened. That day I told you to keep it in your pants, I had no clue she was the job. I didn't know until that fucker shot you. By then, it was too late."

"Too late for what? What the fuck, Joe?"

Joe turned to look at her standing where he left her. Her eyes bore into his soul. His smile was automatic as the words just came out. "Little brother, she owns my heart. I fell in love with her months ago, long before she ever became the job. She is my friend's daughter." His eyes moved to Jason's, and his voice became hard. "And I am fucking in love with her. So, your misplaced anger is nothing compared to what I am going to have to deal with when Mike finds out that I am in love with his daughter. It wouldn't have mattered if you made a move on her. She wouldn't have given you the time of day. She was already in love with me."

"You're so sure of yourself."

Joe laughed, slapping Jason on the shoulder. "So fucking sure. That woman in there will be my wife. She will be the mother of my children. She is going to be your sister-in-law, so you should get over yourself."

"No shit? You're getting married?" Jason looked at Roni, who smiled at him.

"Fucking right I am."

He went to walk back into the loft when Jason said, "Does she know that?"

Joe busted out laughing. "Not yet. But she will."

~

Roni stood there looking at Joe, watching his mouth move. She saw him say the word 'love' and her heart exploded. He was telling his brother that he loved her. No more games, no more worries. This man she was looking at loved her. She knew he would never hurt her. He would never leave her. He was the most honorable man she had ever known. She was finally going to have the life she'd always wanted. But he was so much older than her. Would he want children? Her heart speeding up, she needed to know. She wanted children, at least one.

She watched Joe as he walked back in and right up to her. "I need to talk to you," he said softly. Roni smiled at him and nodded. "Can you guys excuse us for a bit? We need to talk."

Everyone nodded, and the two of them headed back to the bedroom. "We never really talk when we are in this room," she teased.

Joe chuckled. "When we get out of here, we are spending all of our time in the bedroom." He kissed her. "I can't get enough of you."

Roni giggled. "What do we need to talk about?" She stepped away from him, moving to the chair in the corner.

Joe followed her like a puppy and knelt on the floor in front of her. "The jury is deliberating. No one knows how long they'll be, but I want to get out of here before they come back with a verdict. If he gets off, he will be coming for you. So, would you be up for it, to sneak out of here tonight?" She didn't know what to say, or if she could say anything, so she just nodded. "You don't look so sure about this."

"I'm just scared, I suppose. I mean, we are doing this on the pretense that he is getting out. What if he doesn't?"

"It doesn't matter either way. I want to do this with you. I want it to just be us, so we can get to know one another better. Roni, I am serious about this, about us."

She smiled, touching his face. "Joe?"

"Yeah, beautiful?"

"When we get wherever it is that we are going, I'm looking forward to staying in bed with you." She felt the blush cover her from her head to her toes.

Joe kissed her forehead. "You're killing me." Pulling her to her feet, he moved them to the door.

She stopped, turning to look at him. Her hands moved on their own, and before he could protest, she had his jeans undone and was lowering herself to the floor, taking him down her throat in one movement.

Joe's fingers threaded through her hair, gripping it tightly. "Roni, no," he groaned out, his hips pushing forward on their own. "Oh, God." His eyes were glued to her as her head pulled back and pushed forward again, swallowing him again. Five times, she moved on him. He couldn't close his eyes. He couldn't move. He didn't want to move. He wanted to feel this, to see her do this to him.

On the sixth push, her nose touched his stomach and her lips wrapped around the widest part of his cock, and she fucking swallowed. His eyes rolled in his head as she milked him. Stream after stream of cum shot down her throat and filled her mouth, and she swallowed every fucking drop of him. When she pulled back, she spent a few minutes massaging his crown with her teeth, making sure she got every drop of him.

He watched as she pulled back and could see a bit of his cum stringing from him to her lips, but her sweet tongue came out and lapped it up. Carefully, he knelt in front of her. Taking her face in his hands, he covered her mouth with his. No woman had ever been able to make him cum so fast. He didn't want the kiss to end. "So fucking sweet," he whispered on her lips.

"Now, you don't need to die," she whispered as she got up. "Come on, Joe, I'm hungry." As she moved to the door, she turned, watching him stand and tuck his semi-hard cock into his jeans. "So fucking sexy," she mumbled. "Pure sin on legs." Opening the door, she walked out of the room, leaving him standing there.

Roni made it to the living room before Joe grabbed her in his arms, making her squeal, and he laughed. "You are in so much trouble," he whispered in her ear as he set her down. She just laughed and walked over to the couch, sitting next to Becca.

Joe grabbed the phone. "Who wants Chinese?"

"We've got to get back to the office," Jason said.

"I'll talk to you before we head out," Joe told him. Jason nodded, and he and Ben left. Joe looked at Al. "The usual?"

"Yep, listen, Bec and I are heading home in the morning."

"Roni and I are leaving after we eat. I'm taking her down to the islands. It's the only place I can think of where he won't know to look for her. Mike seems to think her mother will tell him about the cabin, so he doesn't want her there."

"Makes sense. You going to call, or are you going to hold the phone all night?"

"Fuck you." Joe laughed. He called and ordered everything on the menu.

When they finished eating, Joe and Roni went and gathered their things. "I'm going to call your father and let him know we are going to disappear."

"Joe, do you think he will figure us out?"

He felt his insides turn over and shook his head in thought. "I'm not sure. I just feel the need to tell him I'm in love with his daughter. If it was me, and you were my daughter, I would want me dead."

She walked up to him, putting her hand on his face. "I think you're wrong. I think my father would be happy for me to have a man such as yourself love me. It's Thanksgiving in a few days. Should we stay for dinner with my parents?"

He laughed. "To be honest, sweetheart, I want nothing to do with your parents. Well, not with your mother anyway."

"What about your family?"

"We do Christmas. I've already been told, if I'm not there, my mother is coming for me." He laughed.

She nodded. "You ready?"

"Hey." He pulled her to him. "Will you come to Christmas dinner with me? I'd like you to meet my mother."

Her smile lit up the room. "I'd love to."

"Then let's go say goodbye. I'll call your father on the way to the airport."

They headed out to say goodbye to Al and Becca, promising to see them in a month at Christmas. Instead of heading out the front with the press, they took the car in the garage. No one was the wiser. As they headed down the highway to the airport, Joe called Mike.

"Mike, it's Joe Blackshaw."

"Joe, how are things going?"

"Well, we are on our way out of town. If this fucker gets off, he is going to make a beeline for her."

"So, you're back on the job?"

Joe chuckled. "Something like that. We decided that the guys being here will make him think she is close. He doesn't know that much about me, and even if he looked, he wouldn't find much."

"Will you be around for Thanksgiving?"

"No, Mike, I'm sorry. Until this is settled, she is in the wind."

"I can't thank you enough, Joe, for doing this for me. I owe you big time. Coming out of retirement to watch over her means the world to me."

Joe looked at Roni. Grabbing her hand, he gave her a gentle squeeze. "I didn't come out of retirement. But you're welcome. I'll have her call you once a week, but it'll be from an unknown number and the calls will be brief."

"I understand. Tell her I love her."

Joe laughed. "Tell her yourself. You're on speaker and she's sitting right here."

"Hi, Daddy."

"Oh, Veronica. You listen to Joe and you do what he tells you to do. He will keep you safe."

She giggled. "You know me, Daddy, I'm not one for taking orders."

"Veronica, please."

"I will. I miss you." Her voice got sad.

"I know. I miss you, too. I'll get in touch with Jason when the verdict comes in. He'll know how to get in touch with you, Joe?"

"Yeah, Mike. I'll keep in touch."

"Thanks, Joe. I owe you. Keep my girl safe."

"I will. Talk soon."

"Yep." Mike disconnected the call.

Roni just sat there with a saddened heart. Her father had no idea that the man he trusted her life with was the man she was in love with.

Joe noticed how quiet she got. He could feel her sadness. Gently, he squeezed her hand as they pulled into the private airport hangar. When he opened the door for her, she just sat there.

"Hey." His voice was soft. "Talk to me."

Roni looked at him. "Is this the best thing to do? If he gets off, I won't ever be able to come home. Joe, this is stupid to run. I know staying here could be dangerous, but he will still be here in a month, in a year. I've been terrified of him for a long time. He is still controlling what I am doing, how I am doing it."

"He's not controlling this, not here and now. I want this time with you."

"Yeah?"

"Oh, hell yeah. Come on, beautiful, let's go relax in the sun."

Smiling, she let him lift her from the truck. They walked hand in hand to the plane.

Joe went to talk to the pilot and then sat with Roni. "Buckle up, our adventure is about to begin." She smiled at him.

Ten minutes later, they were flying down the runway headed to the house they had on St. Bart's in the Caribbean. Roni curled up next to Joe and closed her eyes, falling asleep. Joe rarely slept on planes. He hated the feeling of not being in control. Most of the time, he was too busy with a case to give notice, but now, now he had nothing but time on his hands.

Looking at Roni, he couldn't believe his luck in finding her. He was scared to death of the future, of loving someone like this, but excited to know that the woman next to him would bear his name and his children. Did she even want children? Honestly, it didn't matter to him one way or another. He never wanted to be without her.

Joe closed his eyes, his arm around her, his hand holding her hand.

She was in his soul, embedded for the rest of his life. He knew he was a lucky son-of-a-bitch. Very lucky.

He wasn't sure how long he'd slept when Roni moved away from him, waking him. "What's wrong?"

"I need to use the bathroom. Go back to sleep."

He smiled at her. "I'm good. It's back there. If you want to take a shower, there's one in there."

Bending to kiss him, she whispered on his lips, "I would rather wait for you to join me."

Joe moaned as she kissed him. He leaned over to watch her walk down the aisle. "Damn."

Roni came back and sat on Joe's lap. "So, how much longer until we get to wherever it is you're taking me?" Her voice was soft, her fingers touching his lips.

"I have no idea." His eyes closed as he enjoyed her tender touch.

"Excuse me, Mr. Blackshaw. I have a meal for you both." The flight attendant interrupted them.

Roni giggled and climbed over into her seat. They sat and ate, just smiling, chuckling, and giggling like two young kids in love. That's how Joe felt, like he was a kid again. His eyes sparkled, and his heart finally felt like it was free from any weight his hard and complicated life had put on it.

When their meal was finished, they just sat looking at one another. Joe gently rubbed his thumb across the back of her hand in his. He felt the plane slow down. "We are going to land pretty soon." He was so excited, elated, and then chuckled to himself at the thought that he could be elated. He couldn't seem to stop smiling.

Roni felt terrified at the feelings building in her heart. She wasn't afraid so to speak; she was terrified that she could feel so deeply for someone she hardly knew. The connection between them was so strong, so intense, but yet so comfortable.

"Why do you stare at me the way you do?" she asked softly.

She watched him turn to look at her, trying to hide the trepidation in her eyes. He smiled a kind and gentle smile. "Because you are so beautiful, it scares me."

"I'm not that. My ass is too big. Hell, I'm no model, and I could stand to lose some weight."

"You are perfect, exactly the way you are. I stare at you, as you put it, because I still can't believe you want to be with me. I treated you so badly that first time."

"You did, but it's what I wanted. What I needed."

"Sweetheart, I'll be honest. I haven't been kind to a woman in bed in twenty years. I've never slept with them after, and very few I kissed." He leaned in, whispering, "And not one of them could pull an orgasm from me the way you do. When you walked off that porch, you took a piece of my heart. Hell, you took the whole damn thing. I thought I would go mad with thoughts of you." Reaching up, he touched her face, wiping away the tear that had fallen. "I am so sorry for doing that to you, for treating you so badly."

Roni smiled, kissing his thumb. "I forgive you, and I would really like to have a repeat someday."

"Yeah?"

She nodded, leaning in to kiss him as the pilot announced their descent.

CHAPTER NINE

When they got off the plane, Joe walked them into the office where they had their passports stamped. Roni took hers and looked at it. "So, we are in St. Bart's? Good to know."

Joe laughed, taking her hand, and they walked to the private hangar that housed the jet and loaded their things into the Jeep they kept down there. He helped her into the Jeep, and they were off, laughing and talking all the way to the beach house.

It wasn't a big place—three bedrooms, a living room, and kitchen—but it opened up onto the beach, with a small pool off to the side. Walking in, Roni just stopped and looked at Joe. "Are you kidding me? It's beautiful."

He smiled at her. "Come on, I'll show you where the bedrooms are. I'm not going to assume you are sleeping with me; that is your decision."

"Do you want me to sleep with you?" she asked, teasing him.

"With all that I am, yes, I want you to sleep with me." Grabbing her hand, he pulled her up the few steps to the bedrooms and into the master. "This is our room."

~

Roni stood by the door watching him move through the room. She wanted him, but she wanted to be the seducer, to make love to him. To show him just how she felt about him. No matter how chaotic everything was around them, this between them was perfect.

Joe walked up to her. "I'm going to open some windows. This place has been locked up for a while. Make yourself comfortable." Then he kissed her on the forehead. She turned to watch him walk out the door and down the hall, disappearing into one of the other rooms.

With a smile on her face and devious thoughts running through her head, she moved into the room, dropping her clothes as she walked. By the time she made it to the bed, she was naked. Pulling back the covers, she climbed in, got comfortable, and waited for him to come and find her. She didn't have to wait long. Her eyes locked on his as he made his way to the bed, peeling his clothes off as he did. As he crawled up the bed, he trailed his tongue along the backs of her thighs to her ass, sinking his teeth in the soft flesh, then laving the spot with his tongue. He moved up her back to her mouth and kissed her deeply.

Roni pulled him in while rolling over, managing to end up on top of him. She could feel his erection on her ass as she kissed him. Pushing up a bit, pulling out of the kiss, she looked at him. He was so beautiful with his chiseled jaw and beautiful brown eyes. She loved the wrinkles at his temples, along with whiffs of grey hair. Her fingers touched his face, his eyes, his lips.

Moving down, she lifted herself up, sliding his cock between her legs. His head pressed into her. Flexing her hips, she pushed him inside of her slowly. He was huge, and she knew she was going to hurt herself if she went quickly. As she pushed down, joining his body with hers, she slowly walked her hands down his chest then sat up to slide him deep inside of herself.

"Oh, God." Her moan left her lips as a soft whisper.

Joe's hands gripped her hips to hold her steady, his eyes never leaving hers. Roni could feel the goose flesh cover her when he slipped the rest of the way in, her body taking him to the end of her core.

"So fucking sweet," Joe moaned as he watched her nipples harden, felt her pulse around him while she came, her eyes slightly rolling in her head.

Roni didn't move once she came. Her eyes locked on him. "What was that?" Her eyes questioned him. "Did you feel that?"

With a shy smile, he whispered to her, his fingers pressed into her ass. "It was an orgasm." His thumbs pressed on her pubic bone. "Yes, beautiful." He shifted and she moaned. "I felt it."

They looked at one another with lust laden eyes. A small smile crossed her lips as she rocked forward then back on him. "Joe, oh God," she moaned as she moved.

Joe wanted to close his eyes and savor this beautiful woman, but he knew, if he did, he was going to come. She felt incredible to him. He held her hips while her body slinked like a snake back and forth. With her back arching, her perfect tits gently swayed with each movement. He wanted nothing more than to stay hard for her. After a few movements, he synced his thrusts with hers and they made love. It was so surreal for him. He had never felt like this, felt this from a woman.

"Joe," she moaned. He could feel her tighten against his cock again. Her silken walls contracted slowly around him. He felt her swollen bud rubbing gently on his bone each time he pushed up. "Joe, oh God." She was coming, and he needed to stay hard for her, but he was finding it very difficult.

"Come on, beautiful. Come for me."

"Mmm," she moaned, and that was all it took for him to release with her. Sitting up as her head fell back, her back arching, he clamped down on her nipple, his hands holding her as they came hard together.

Pulling herself upright, her hands holding his face, she kissed him. Joe moved his hands into her hair, pulling her flush to his chest as he deepened the kiss. When they separated, he looked deep into her sedate eyes.

"Marry me." The words were so natural to say; they felt so right. "Marry me, Roni. Let me love you for the rest of my life."

Her smile was slow, her eyes filling with tears. "Yes," she whispered.

Joe rolled so they were laying in each other's arms. "Yeah?"

She nodded. "Yes."

He pulled her to his chest. "I love you," he whispered against her forehead.

Closing their eyes, they fell asleep wrapped around each other.

Their slumber was short but sound. Slowly, his body woke to a new feeling, a new feeling of completeness. The woman in his arms was what had been missing all his life. He knew now what Al felt; he understood why leaving to spend his life with Becca was all that mattered to him. His fingers caressed up and down her spine. When they reached her ass, he cupped it. His heart leaped at the plumpness, the sheer fullness of her. She fit so perfectly within his embrace as if God himself molded her just for him. Nothing was ever going to change this. He felt himself growing hard just thinking about loving her. When her hand moved up his chest, Joe rolled them over, slowly kissing her as he pulled her leg over his hip and pushed inside of her.

"Mmm, God, Joe."

Smiling, he made love to her for what felt like hours. They loved each other with gentle touches, sweet caresses, and deep kisses. Her orgasms came one after the other, her body covered in a sweet sheen of sweat as he pulled them from her. Her mews became the music of his life, her scent the fragrance of the Gods, and her taste, the ambrosia he would live off for the rest of his life. Slipping his hand between them, he gently pinched her swollen bud between his fingers, sending her body into shock as she screamed out, her orgasm shaking her to her core. Joe could do nothing but watch her face, feel her body and release. He was owned, completely and utterly owned.

~

Roni lay in his arms feeling like she had never felt before. He had just made love to her. With her body still humming, the smile across her face made her cheeks hurt. Could any person be this happy? She knew nothing about him, nor did he know anything about her. But in this bed, none of that seemed to matter. She needed to know if he wanted children.

"Joe?" She spoke softly.

"Yeah, beautiful?"

"I know this is putting the cart before the horse, but I need to know something."

He chuckled. "Sweetheart, the cart is long gone. It's so far ahead of us I can't see it anymore."

"I suppose, but, Joe?" She raised her head to look at him. "Do you want children? Because I want children, at least one."

She closed her eyes as his hand touched her face. "Yes, Roni, I want to have children with you."

"Thank you."

Chuckling, he pulled her in for a kiss. "How about we get you cleaned up, and I'll make us something to eat? Then we can go exploring."

"Mmm, I could eat." Roni took a shower while Joe made them something light to eat. Together, they spent the day walking along the beach, talking and laughing, just learning about one another.

As they lay in each other's arms after making love again, Joe was feeling incredible at how much they were similar yet different. He could never have imagined that he would ever meet someone like her. "Roni." His whisper was warm on her face.

Her eyes slowly opened to look at him. "Mmm," she moaned, kissing him.

"I want to marry you, sooner rather than later. Will you marry me?"

"Yes," she whispered against his lips. "Yes, Joe, I will marry you."

With his hand in her hair, he deepened the kiss. "Tomorrow? Will you marry me tomorrow?"

Her hand wrapped around his semi-hard cock. "Yes."

Chuckling, Joe let her work him into a full erection before he half-fucked her, half-made love to her. When they were finished, the air in the bedroom smelled of sex, and the sheets and blankets were destroyed.

Neither of them wanted to move or get up and clean themselves or the bed. They lay in their sex-exhausted comas, loving the feel of one another. It was Roni who made the effort to move.

"Mmm, where are you going?" Joe moaned as she tried to move away from him. He pulled her back against his chest.

"I have to use the bathroom. I'm a mess."

He chuckled, pulling her on top of him. "Oh, I know you are. Kiss me first."

Kiss him she did, leveling him and leaving him breathless as she climbed off him and off the bed. Turning his head, he watched her walk to the bathroom with his cum slowly running down her inner thighs. His heart tightened in his chest at the realization of how much he had fallen so deeply in love with her. She was an incredible human being. So smart, funny, sassy, and probably the most incredible lover he had ever known.

His thoughts interrupted when she called out to him. "Joe, do you want to take a shower with me?"

Chuckling, he pulled himself up and headed to shower only to see her soaking wet and naked. Pulling his lip between his teeth, he walked into the shower, his hands coming up to cup her breasts. "So fucking sweet," he moaned as he devoured her. They stayed in the shower loving one another until the water ran cold.

CHAPTER TEN

The next morning when they woke, they didn't make love. Instead, they got dressed and headed to the airport to fly to the Dominican Republic. The trip took most of the day, but when they returned, they were husband and wife.

Walking up to the door, Joe opened it, carrying Roni over the threshold and straight to the bedroom. As he climbed on the bed with her, she ended up sitting on his thighs. Wrapping his hands around her head, he whispered. "You are mine now. My wife. I love you, beautiful."

Giggling, Roni kissed him. "Fucking right I am, and you are mine, Joe Blackshaw, and don't you forget it."

He laid her back with a sexy grin. "Not in a million fucking years. Now, can I make love to my wife?"

"Oh, God, yes please."

Hours later, banging on the door woke Joe. Pulling himself away from her, he threw on his jeans and made his way to the door. Standing outside was a policeman.

"Mr. Joe Blackshaw?"

"Yeah, is everything all right?"

"We got a call from a man named Al Blackshaw. He said he's your brother, and he has been trying to get in touch with you for a few days now. He needs you to call home. Something about a family emergency."

Joe's heart stopped. It was hard for him to swallow. He felt Roni walk up behind him. The policeman looked around him. "Are you Veronica Holloway?"

Roni didn't know what was going on, and the man freaked her out, so she shook her head no. He nodded and looked at Joe.

"Thank you, sir. I'll call home." He shook the man's hand and then shut the door, turning to look at Roni. "Something's wrong. No one knows where we are. Come on." He took her hand and led her back to the bedroom, back to the closet. When they walked in, he hit a button on the wall that Roni hadn't noticed, and a steel door closed behind them.

She smiled at him. "Do you have a safe room in every house you own?"

He chuckled. "Every damn one of them. We used these houses to protect people. They are necessary." Kissing her on the forehead, he moved around her. Walking to the back of the closet, he slid a panel away and clicked on all the monitors. Then he turned on his phone. "Shit."

"What?" Roni walked up behind him.

"My phone is dead." He went to his bag which he hadn't really unpacked and pulled out his changer, plugging it in. He set it down and then went back to the monitors, back to where Roni stood looking at them.

Joe was pushing buttons, and each button turned on a different camera. Then he turned on the sensors, which turned on the cameras if someone or something moved in front of them. Looking at each screen, his heart rate started to slow. There was no one around.

"Do you think he found us?" Her voice sounded almost childlike.

When Joe turned to her, he could see nothing but fear in her eyes. Pulling her to his chest, he wrapped his arms around her. "There is no way he could find us."

"Then why are we in this room?" She tightened her grip on his waist.

"Because it's better to be safe than sorry." He eyed the monitors as his phone sprung to life. He saw the missed calls, the messages. Letting go of Roni, he called Al.

"Jesus fucking Christ, Joe. I've been trying to find you for five days. We have a serious problem here."

"Here? I thought you and Bec went back to the cabin?"

"Listen, brother, are you sitting down?"

"Just fucking say it, Al." His insides were churning, his hands trembling. Taking a deep breath, he waited.

"You need to come back. I can't do this on the phone. You need to get your ass back here and now. I'll meet you at Mom's. It's bad."

"Just fucking tell me," he shouted, but the line was dead.

"What's wrong?" Roni asked softly as Joe put the phone down.

He couldn't breathe. Picking his head up, he said as calmly as he could, "We need to leave. We need to get to Chicago." He was surprised by her reaction. She turned and put her things in her bag, as well as his.

"Then let's go." She knew his mother lived in Chicago with his little brother. "Come on, Joe, let's go." She put her hand out to take his.

He stood there looking at her, looking at her hand. Pulling the phone plug out of the wall, he picked up the phone, shut off the monitors, and took her hand. Neither of them said a word on the way to the airport or on the flight. Joe didn't let go of her hand until they landed in Chicago. Standing on the tarmac, he pulled her into him. "Thank you."

She snuggled into him. "Don't thank me. I love you."

He kissed the top of her head. "I love you."

After going through customs, they headed to his mother's house. Pulling up, Joe could see an extra car in the driveway. He knew there should have been more. He was finding it difficult to swallow, difficult to breathe.

Roni sat and looked at him. "Hey, you all right?"

"Something is wrong. I don't know if I can do this." His eyes moved to the door as it opened. Al came walking out. Joe could see the anger in his eyes, the devastation on his face. "Fuck," Joe whispered.

He got out of the truck and walked around to open Roni's door, but she met him at the bumper. "I'm right here, Joe."

Nodding, they headed toward Al. As they moved closer, Joe could see the tears in his eyes. Becca walked out behind him, her face red, running and throwing herself into Joe's chest with a heart-wrenching sob. His eyes never left Al's. Holding Roni's hand and half-carrying Becca, he moved closer. Watching his brother move toward him, Roni let go of his hand, and Joe let go of Becca as Al wrapped him in his embrace.

"God, brother," he choked out through his tears. "I am so glad to see you alive."

Joe's brain wasn't computing. Why wouldn't they be alive? He moved to pull away, but Al wouldn't let him go. "What happened?" His voice was full of anger. "What the hell happened, Al?"

"They're gone, Joe. They are fucking gone."

His heart stopped. He couldn't breathe. "Who? Who the fuck is gone?" His eyes shifted to Roni, whose face was wet from her tears. Becca had her arm wrapped around her. "Let me go, Al." He tried to pull away again. "Let me the fuck go." Hesitantly, Al let him go. "Now, tell me what the fuck you're talking about."

"Sherry, Jason, Ben, and Stellar are dead. Murdered," Al said softly.

Joe stood there, the ringing in his ears so loud he thought he would go crazy. He watched his brother's mouth moving, but he couldn't hear a fucking word he was saying. It was Roni who stepped forward and touched his chest. He shifted his eyes to her, looking at her with eyes full of hate, so much so that she took a step back away from him. She took another step and then another. Becca was horrified to watch what was happening. Roni then turned and started walking down the street.

Joe stood there unable to move. "Stop her," Becca cried urgently.

His eyes shifted to her then back to Roni; she was moving fast. Before he knew what was happening, his feet were chasing after her.

He grabbed her around the waist, pulling her to his chest. "No. No, beautiful. No." When she put her head back, against his chest, he let out the breath he was holding. "I can't lose you. I won't. I'm so sorry."

"It's all my fault, isn't it?" She sounded devastated.

"No, beautiful, it's not your fault. You didn't do this."

"Joe, I'm so sorry. If you didn't know my father, none of this would have happened."

"We don't know what happened. Come back to the house with me. I need you with me. I can't do this alone. Roni, I've never needed anyone more than I need you right now. Please, baby." His voice dropped. "I need my wife."

She turned in his arms, her hand touching his face, wiping his tears. "I'm so sorry."

He nodded, pulling her to him, holding her, hugging her. "Come on." Turning, they walked back to where Al and Becca were waiting for them. Then they went inside the house where Joe's mother and youngest brother were. His mother was visibly upset. Joe went to her, grabbing her in a hug.

"Oh, Joey. Am I going to outlive all my children?" She sobbed into his chest.

"No, Mom. I'm here, and I'm fine. Al is fine, and Alex is fine. Do you know what happened?"

She shook her head as he helped her sit. Joe sat next to his mother, holding her hand, looking at Al. "What happened?"

Al looked at Roni for a long time. "I don't have all the details yet. Sherry had her throat slit. Ben was shot three times in the chest, as was Stellar. Jason was tortured. From what I was told, three of his fingers were cut off, and he had multiple stab wounds in his thighs. The detective on the case said one of them severed the femoral artery, and ultimately, he bled out, but not before he suffered. The place was ransacked. They wouldn't let me in there to see what was missing but, considering what happened next, I can guess."

Roni looked at him with tears on her cheeks. "What happened next?"

Joe reached over and grabbed her hand. Becca came to sit next to her. "Roni, your father is in intensive care, critical condition, fighting for his life. The maid found him in his home office in D.C. He was tortured the same way as Jason."

Her head snapped to look at Joe. "Tony. This was Tony. Oh my God."

Letting go of his mother's hand, he pulled Roni to his chest. "I'm so sorry, beautiful."

His mother smiled a small smile, knowing her oldest son had finally found happiness. "I'm so happy for you, Joey," she said quietly.

Joe turned to look at her. "Mom, this is Roni, my wife."

"No shit. You got married?" Al didn't really seem surprised by the news.

He looked at Al. "What do you think was taken?"

"The file on all the houses, all the safe room access codes. That's why I sent the police to find you. I called the sheriff in every city we have a house. Joe, he is coming, and he is coming with a vengeance. We have to protect her."

"The fucking bastard is going to pay with his life for this. How the hell did he get off?"

"Self-defense. I personally think the judge was in his pocket. But he got off, and now he has killed five people."

"What about my mother?"

"She claims she has no idea what is going on."

Looking at Joe, she spoke softly. "My mother was there. She has a weird thing for Tony. I'm sure she watched the whole thing." She turned to Al. "How long ago did all of this happen?"

Al looked at his mother. "Four days ago. The police came to tell Mom, and then Alex called me. I've been looking for you since."

Joe nodded. "I need a few minutes. Excuse me." He got up and headed through the house to the back door. They all sat there and watched him walk out.

~

Roni turned to Al. "I need to see my father."

"No. You cannot go anywhere near him. Tony will know that's where you are going. He'll be waiting for you."

"Well, if you think he doesn't know right where I'm at then you are an idiot. I'm not leading that fucker right to your mother. We need to leave. I need to leave. It's me he wants. I won't be responsible for another member of your family being murdered." She stood.

"Roni, don't make me lock you in the safe room because I will. You need to talk this over with Joe. You can't just go running around out there alone."

She laughed. "I'm not going running around. I'm going home to see my mother. I'm sure Tony will be there waiting for me, and if he's not, he'll be there shortly after. My mother is in bed with that sick bastard, I'm sure of it."

Joe's mom was smiling. "I like her. She's a good match for Joey. He needs someone who's not afraid to stand up to him."

Smiling, Roni looked at her. "Thank you. Joe doesn't scare me. He might think he does, but I lived with the devil himself for over a year. You can't get much scarier than that."

His mother chuckled. "You've never seen Joey angry, have you?"

Roni giggled. "Oh, yes, I have."

Becca laughed. "She holds her own, Sally."

Joe came walking back in to see nothing but fire in Roni's eyes. He knew that look, one of her many looks. "What?" he asked with a slight smile on his lips. He loved the different expressions that flew through her eyes. He couldn't wait to spend his life figuring them all out.

"I want to go home. I'm going to have a hard time living with myself after what he did to your family. I know my mother is in on this as well, and if he isn't there, he will be after I get there."

"No!" Joe shouted, making everyone jump. "You are not going anywhere near them, not now, not tomorrow, not next week. No, Roni, it isn't going to happen."

"Just because I am your wife doesn't mean you own me."

"Oh, sweetheart, it most certainly does. I'm putting my foot down. You are not going."

Roni shocked everyone when she busted out laughing. "I hate to tell you this, Mr. Blackshaw, but I am thirty years old. I will do what I want, when I want, and with whomever I want." She screamed at him, "You do not own me!"

Joe reached over and grabbed her, picking her up. Roni fought him as he carried her up the stairs and into a room, kicking the door closed. He turned and pressed her against the door, putting all his weight into her body, pinning her. "You are not going anywhere." His voice was rough.

"I am going." Her voice came out raspy.

His eyes filled with tears, and he dropped his head on her chest, letting them go. Roni held him close, her fingers tender as they moved through his hair. "I've got you, husband. I love you so much, Joe. You must let me do this. We have to draw him out into the open. You know I'm the only bait we have."

Shaking his head, he tried to argue. "I can't lose you. I won't lose you."

"You won't let him take me. You won't let him hurt me. I know that."

"I would have laid every penny I had on the fact that he wouldn't be able to take down Jason or Ben, but he did." Picking his head up, she wiped his tears. "He murdered my brothers, beautiful. I won't let him near you."

"He won't get near me, and if he does, I know you will find me."

"Roni, please, don't make me do this. We can find another way."

"Joe, you know a great many people. You still have thirty men working for your company, and you know the police. We can draw him out and you know it. I know you're scared, because I'm terrified. But you know what?" Joe shook his head. He hated that she was making sense. "I am not going to let that fucker have control over me again. I want to be married to you. I want a life with you." She leaned in and whispered, "I want babies Joe. We can't have babies if we're on the run. We need to end him."

"Impossible. You are an impossible woman."

She giggled. "Why? Because you know I'm right?"

He didn't want to admit it, because he was terrified that she was going to die, but she was right. She was the only bait they had. "Yes."

Her smile nearly broke her face. "What? Don't tell me the great Joe Blackshaw is admitting defeat?"

He chuckled. "I am conceding to the fact that you are correct. Not defeat, simply because there is no contest."

"I love you," she whispered on his lips as she kissed him.

His hands moved to her hair, threading his fingers in it so he could control something, anything. Joe wasn't used to conceding anything to anyone, especially the woman he loved. But he knew he couldn't keep her locked away, and he certainly couldn't control her. She wasn't going to stand for that. These facts just embedded her deeper into his soul.

"We need to go back downstairs and make a plan."

When they walked into the living room, his mother smiled at him. "She is good for you, Joey."

"Yeah, Mom, she is. Now, we have things to do. Roni, you need to call your mother. We need to find out where she is. Let her know you are on your way to D.C. to see your dad. That way, if Tony is in L.A., he will head that way." Turning, he looked at Al. "We need to get into her parents' house. It's going to take everyone to do this. Tell them to hide in every fucking place they can find, inside and out. We need visual and audio. No communication once they are in play. We all move as one." Al nodded to him.

Roni pulled out her phone. "Put it on speaker," Joe said to her. "Everyone, quiet." Joe watched as everyone turned off their phones. He nodded to Roni. "Tell her you were in L.A. and we are on our way to D.C."

She nodded and sent the call through. No one was breathing as the phone rang. "Veronica? My God, I've been trying to reach you. Where are you? Your father has been horribly hurt."

"I know, Mom. I'm on my way to D.C. now. Which hospital is he in?"

"Wait, where are you? Where have you been?"

"I've been with Joe Blackshaw. Didn't daddy tell you? We've been in L.A. I'm sitting in a plane on the tarmac. What happened to Daddy?"

"Someone broke into the house in D.C. and attacked him. He's at Walter Reed. Is Joe with you now?"

"Yes, he's been keeping me safe. Are you at the hospital?"

"No, I'm at the house in D.C. Why don't you come here before you go to the hospital? Then we can ride over together."

"All right, but I have to go, Mom. We're getting ready to take off. I'll see you soon." Roni disconnected the call and turned off her phone. Looking up, Joe saw the hatred in her eyes, something he hoped he would never see directed toward him. "I'm not going to D.C. I'll go when that fucker is dead."

Joe didn't take his eyes from her when he said, "Al, call the crew. Roni, what is the security code to the house?" She gave him the code, their eyes locked. "Bec, I need you to take my mom and Alex to your cabin. I know you have a safe room there. Please don't hesitate to use it."

Becca looked at Al, and he nodded to her as he pulled her into his arms. "Please come back," she whispered through her tears.

"I promise." He kissed her. "I love you. I will see you soon."

Al walked everyone out to the car, while Joe and Roni sat staring at each other. "I just found you. I'm so scared, Roni. I can't let you do this."

Shaking her head, she reminded him, "I'm the only one who can do this. As long as I know you are there, I can do this. I know you won't let him hurt me."

He got up and went to sit next to her, taking her hands in his. "I will give my life to save you."

"No, don't you dare, Joe Blackshaw. I can't nor do I want to live in this world without you. We can't doubt ourselves. We need to be positive, stay strong; otherwise, he will win. No mistakes, Joe. No heroics. Do your job. I'm the job."

"You are my wife."

"Not when we leave this house. I am the job. It's the only way this is going to work. If he thinks I am anything more, he will kill you, or me."

"She's right, Joe, and you know it," Al said from behind him.

Joe closed his eyes. "I know." Looking at Roni, he ground out, "You do everything I tell you. No arguing, no questions asked, understood?" She nodded. "I won't lose you. I become a different man when I work, so just remember that I love you and whatever I say or do is the job."

"Okay."

"Good, now let's get moving. We have to get to the house, and L.A. is a long way away."

"I chartered a plane for Becca and Mom, and one for us. Let's go," Al said.

Roni stood up and Joe pulled her into his arms. "Every word I say, you hear?"

Smiling, she tipped her head up. "I hear you."

As they flew across the country, Joe and Al made all the arrangements. They had gained access to the house and set all the cameras in place. As each one came online, the video feeds popped up on the laptops they had. Roni sat there watching the brothers work in tandem, like a perfect ballet.

Her fear was so overwhelming that she couldn't do or say anything. Deep inside, she knew that Tony was going to kill her; she just didn't understand how someone could snap like that. He was an asshole, yes, and he was brutal. But a murderer? She just couldn't wrap her head around it.

When she refocused her eyes, she looked up at Joe. He was watching her again. She smiled a small smile as he mouthed 'I love you' to her. Giving him a slight nod, she turned her head to look out the window. She needed to get a grip. This wasn't a game. Her and Joe's lives were at stake here. If anything happened to Al, Becca would never forgive her. Not to mention their mother. God, she'd lost a daughter and two sons.

She felt something on her hand. Looking down, she saw a tear that had fallen. Joe watched her wipe her cheek before moving to sit next to her.

"Hey, you all right?" His voice sounded soft and kind.

"He murdered your brothers. How am I ever going to be all right? I'm so sorry, Joe."

He pulled her into his arms. "I know, beautiful. We can grieve when we end this fucker. Right now, my job, as you put it, is to end him, and I'm going to. We are going to."

The captain came over the speaker to announce their arrival in L.A. Joe sat her back in her seat, and she buckled her seatbelt. When the plane landed, they got in a black SUV and headed to her family home.

When they pulled up, the house looked vacant. They put in the passcode, and the gates opened as Al got out of the car. Roni wanted to know everything that was going on, but they thought it best she didn't; that way she looked natural.

Walking in the house felt eerie for her. She knew there were at least thirty men hidden, not including the police and S.W.A.T. team. But everything looked normal. Nothing was out of place, and no one was visible. She should have felt safe, secure, but she didn't. She wanted to touch Joe, but she couldn't show any attachment to him or Tony would for sure kill him.

"Call your mom. Tell her there was a problem with the plane and you couldn't get on a domestic flight." She nodded, turning on her phone. "Speaker," he said.

"Veronica, I thought you were on your way here?"

"There was a problem with the plane, and all the domestic flights were booked. I can't get a flight out until morning, so I'm at the house."

"Is Joe Blackshaw with you?"

"Yeah. I'll be there tomorrow afternoon. I'm tired, Mom, so I'm just going to go to bed. How's Daddy?"

"He's doing better. Listen, I'm going to send the plane back for you. Get some rest. It will be there in five hours."

Roni looked at Joe. "Okay, thanks, Mom." Disconnecting the call, she said, "She has never been this nice to me. Why does she keep asking me if you are with me?"

"I can guess. All right, so we have five hours before they get here. Why don't you go get some sleep? I'll keep watch."

She nodded and headed upstairs with Joe behind her. When she walked into her room, she stopped short. Her room had been ransacked. Turning to look at Joe, he put his finger to his mouth to shush her. He nodded for her to move behind him as he walked through her room, and she stayed inches behind him. Her closet was completely destroyed, her clothes shredded. Nothing was left on the hangers, and the drawers were pulled out and thrown about.

"What the fuck," she whispered.

Joe moved to the door. Pushing it shut, he grabbed her and pulled her into his embrace. "I got you," he whispered when he realized she was shaking.

"My mother did this. She hates me."

"Come on, beautiful. Try to get some sleep. I'll be right here."

He pulled away from her and opened the door. Roni stepped out of the closet only to stop in her tracks. Tony was standing in the doorway. Joe was still in the closet, unseen by him.

"What the fuck are you doing here?" She made her voice as calm as possible.

"You fucking fat ass bitch. I'm here to finish what I was hired to do," he snapped. Joe hit the panic button in his pocket and pulled his gun from behind him.

"What are you talking about?" Her voice was still calm. She knew he wasn't going to hurt her, not with Joe behind her.

"You know, when your mother asked me to fucking marry you, I nearly threw up. But she promised to split everything with me. The only thing that was good about you was that fucking tight cunt of yours that first time. Since then, I've literally had to stop myself from vomiting every time I fucked you."

She just stood there, trying to control her temper. She wasn't afraid of him anymore. He was trying to deflate her, lessen who she was. Taking a deep breath, she looked around the room. "Did you do this?"

He laughed. "Your fucking father refused to tell me where you were. Your mother is making sure he doesn't recover, and if you are gone, then everything will go to her by default."

Roni crinkled her eyebrows at him. "What are you talking about?"

"Your father changed his will. When he dies, you get everything, and your fucking whore of a mother gets nothing. She hired me to marry you, then she would kill your father, I would kill you, and we would split the fortune. God, you are so fucking stupid. Do you really think that I would be with a woman who looks like you, with your fat ass and those fat fucking tits of yours? You are a disgusting example of a woman."

Joe stood behind her, wanting with all that he was to touch her, to let her know she was none of those things. But they needed him to admit to everything he'd done.

Roni squared her shoulders. "Did you kill Jason Blackshaw?"

Tony chuckled. "Fucking asshole thought he was so tough. He crumpled like a rag doll. The fucking pussy begged me not to kill him. He should have told me where you were."

"I was upstairs, you fucking idiot. Tony, you are going to jail for the rest of your life."

"Not before I finish my contract with your fucking mother. It should net me a nice chunk of change to pay for a good lawyer. Self-defense."

"Exactly how are you going to use self-defense?" She knew she needed to keep him talking, and she knew that every word was being recorded. There were men in this room and right outside this room.

"That fucker attacked me right downstairs. Your mother saw it all.

He came after me when I stopped by the office to see if he knew where you were."

She shook her head. "You really are fucking stupid. What did the secretary do?"

"Call me fucking stupid again, you fat fucking bitch, and I will show you..."

Roni cut him off. She was pissed now. "Or you'll show me what, Tony? You'll show me how hard you can hit? I'm still fucking here. Are you going to show me how much of a fucking lame fuck you are? You're going to show me what, Tony? Come on, you mother fucker. Come on!!!" She screamed at him. She could see the fury in his eyes, on his face. "What's the matter, Tony? You fucking scared?"

"Fuck you!" he screamed as he stepped forward, raising his hand.

Roni saw the gun. "Fucking do it, Tony. Do it!" she screamed at him.

The next ten seconds moved in slow motion as Tony stepped forward again. Joe wrapped his arm around her waist, stepping into her and turning his back to shield her as Tony fired the gun. The bullet sliced Joe's arm, hitting the door frame. The next thing she remembered was the gunshots. Eight, maybe ten in all, and then a thud.

Joe stepped into the closet, kicking the door shut. He stumbled and fell to his knees, taking her with him. The weight of his body knocked her onto the floor, with him on top of her.

"I love you," he whispered.

Roni tried to get up, but he weighed too much. Struggling, she started to scream. "Joe! Joe!"

The door flew open, and she screamed again. His weight was lifted off her, and she turned over as Al laid him down. "No! No! Oh God, Joe!" Her screams continued as she looked at the blood that covered him. Her eyes shifted to Al. "God, please help him."

Two men came rushing in. Al moved out of the way, picking up Roni to move her so they could work on him. She fought him. "Come on, let them work on him," Al said as he watched.

"He's got a pulse," one man said.

"Roll him over so I can see the damage," another ordered.

"Shit." He turned to look at Al then grabbed some bandages. "One went through, but the second one is still in there." He put a stethoscope to his chest. "Fuck, we need to get him to the hospital. He has a collapsed lung."

Al backed up with his arm wrapped around Roni while they worked to get Joe ready to be transported. Two other guys came in, and they put him on a stretcher and carried him out into her room. She fought with Al to get away, but he held on to her.

"Let me go, Al."

"No, Roni, you need to let them work on him."

"I'm fucking going with him. I'm not leaving him. Let me go. If he dies, I am going to be there." She was hysterical, gasping for breath.

Al let her go. She nearly collapsed, her legs were shaking so bad. Al helped her out into her room as they were lifting Joe to take him down to the ambulance. He didn't let her go as they followed. Once they had him in the ambulance, Al helped her inside.

"I'll meet you there," he said to her.

She didn't answer him, her eyes locked on Joe and the blood pouring out of his chest where the bullet went through. The two men worked on him, starting an IV, applying bandages. It seemed like minutes when the ambulance doors opened, and they were taking him away. Roni followed the best she could, but they were running.

She had no idea what was happening or how long she had been sitting on the floor crying when Al found her. Squatting down in front of her, he touched her arm. "Roni, come on, sweetheart. Joe is in surgery. Becca is on her way."

Roni nodded at him while he helped her stand. With his arm around her, they made their way to the waiting room. She sat in a trance for hours. Becca had come and was sitting next to her, holding her while she silently cried.

After everything she had lived through, she had finally found him, and now she wasn't so sure he was going to survive. Could she handle this? Remembering how she felt when they were apart for the few months, and now knowing that he loved her, she wasn't so sure. "I can't do this."

The door opened, and a doctor walked in. "Are you the family of Joe Blackshaw?"

Al stood up. "I'm his brother. This is his wife." He turned to Roni.

The doctor looked at her. "Mrs. Blackshaw."

She couldn't breathe. The ringing in her ears was so loud. She was gasping for air, and then nothing. She passed out, slamming face first onto the floor.

"Oh my God!" Becca yelled. "Al, help her."

Al bent and picked her up, and her face was bloody. "Jesus Christ." He looked at the doctor.

"Bring her." He turned and opened the door, holding it for Al. "Follow me." He rushed into a room. "Put her on the bed." Al laid her down, moving away while the doctor examined her. "She has a broken nose. I want to get a C.T. scan to make sure everything is all right." He moved out of the room, yelling for a nurse.

Al and Becca stood there in shock as they wheeled her out of the room. "Doc," Al said as he was leaving. "My brother?"

"Walk with me." Al and Becca followed him out the door. "It was touch and go. We lost him twice during surgery. The bullet that passed through him shattered his shoulder blade. But the second one hit his lung. It was difficult to get out. He lost a great deal of blood, but I'm hopeful he will make a full recovery. He's in recovery but will be moved to I.C.U., down on the second floor." The doctor stopped walking. "I have him in a drug-induced coma. It's going to be a struggle for him to breathe. You can go down and see him in about an hour."

"We'll wait here for Roni," Becca said.

"I'll be back," the doctor said as he moved away from them.

Al turned to Becca. "Jesus, Bec." He pulled her into his arms. "All he wanted was to have some happiness and now all of this."

"He was protecting her."

"I should have shot the fucker after the first shot. We needed to get him to confess. Roni did a great job. I can't even imagine how scared she was."

"When you love someone like she loves Joe, you find the strength. Come on, let's go sit. You need to call your mom and Alex. They're at the loft."

He hugged her for a few minutes longer, and then they went back to the waiting room where Al called his mother and brother. Alex was bringing them over to the hospital.

An hour later, the doctor came in. "Mrs. Blackshaw is going to be fine. We got the bullet out, and she has a broken nose and a fractured malar."

"Wait, what bullet?" Al was shocked.

"I'm not sure, but she had a bullet in her shoulder. It was between the bones, so there was no damage."

Becca looked at the doctor. "Malar? Is that the cheekbone?"

"Yes. We have her in recovery next to her husband. I'm going to try to keep them in the same room, but because Joe needs so much attention, I'm not sure I can pull that off right now."

Al stood there in shock. His brother was in a coma, Roni shot. "When can we see them?" He wasn't even sure he'd said it.

"Come with me, I'll take you to Joe's room."

They followed the doctor like zombies. Neither Becca or Al could comprehend that Roni had been shot. His mother and brother were in the waiting room. The reunion was less than happy. Al filled them in on what he knew of Joe and Roni. The four of them sat there not saying a word. Al held Becca's hand, giving it a squeeze every now and then.

After some time had passed, a nurse walked in, taking Al first to Joe's room. He had to grab hold of the door frame when he saw him lying in the bed, covered in bandages, with tubes attached to him, a ventilator down his throat. "Fuck."

"It always looks worse than what it is. The lines are for fluids and drainage. The doctor has him in a drug-induced coma. There was extensive damage to his lung. He nearly lost it. It's going to be a long road to recovery, but we are confident that he will recover. Come on in, sit and talk to him. I like to think that patients in comas can hear what is going on around them, so talking to them, reading to them is always a good thing."

Al slowly walked to his bed. "What the fuck, Joe? Always the hero." He chuckled as he wiped his tears. "Mom is going to be so pissed at you. She's here, in the waiting room with Bec and Alex."

His heart rate sped up a little. Al looked at the nurse, and she smiled at him. "See, I think he can hear you."

CHAPTER ELEVEN

The days ran together in a blur over the next week. Roni still hadn't woken up, and the doctors were ready to wake Joe from his coma. He was healing faster than they anticipated. Al, Becca, Sally, and Alex all stood at the foot of his bed watching as they moved Roni over, so the doctors and nurses could work.

First, they stopped the drip of medicine that was keeping him asleep. "It should take a few minutes before the medicine releases its hold and he begins to wake. Al, why don't you come over to this side, so he can see you? He is going to struggle with the tube in his throat."

Al moved to the other side. "Can't you take out the tube?"

"It will be a gradual thing. We need to wean him off, adding less and less pressure so he can rebuild the strength and use of his lung."

Al didn't take his eyes off him. He could see his eyes moving behind his eyelids, then those lids fluttered. It was natural for him to move his hand up to the tube in his mouth. Al gently stopped him. "No, buddy. Just relax. We're here." Joe's eyes opened, looking right at him. Al saw the fear in them. "It's over. He's dead. You got this, brother." His voice cracked, and Becca came over, resting her hand on Al's back. "You're in the hospital. You were shot. Just relax."

Becca reached up and wiped a tear from Joe's eye. "Roni is fine." He closed his eyes and relaxed, squeezing Al's hand.

"We aren't going anywhere. I'm here. You have to keep the ventilator on for a few days. One of the bullets tore up your lung. Let yourself heal, buddy. Let yourself heal."

Becca grabbed a chair for their mother, who came to take Al's place. It broke Becca's heart to know that two of her sons had died at the hands of that monster, and now another lay in the bed fighting for his life. She sat there for hours holding his hand, crying silent tears.

When the doctor was finished checking him over, Roni was moved back next to Joe's bed. Becca wanted Joe to know she was there with him, so she managed to put Roni's hand in Joe's. His eyes opened, looking at her. Becca knew Joe could sense something was wrong. A tear rolled down the side of his face. His mother softly told him, "She's alive, Joey. Sleeping but alive. You heal. She is going to need you."

As the days passed, Joe's ventilator was used less and less, his lung growing stronger. The doctor had come in, moving Roni away. She still hadn't woken up.

"Okay, Joe. We're going to take the ventilator off today. You are healing nicely and have been breathing pretty much on your own for the last twenty-four hours. It's going to be a little uncomfortable, and your throat is going to be sore. Talking will be difficult so try not to talk a great deal."

Joe blinked his eyes. Everyone left the room and waited in the hallway while the doctor removed the tube. When they went back in, Roni was next to his bed again. Joe's eyes were wide open.

"What happened?" His voice came out as a raspy, soft whisper.

"Well, he got three shots off. One was a through and through, and one sliced your arm, but the other tore the top half of your lung to shit. He's dead. I emptied my clip into him."

"Roni?"

Al's eyes moved to her still body in the bed next to Joe's. "We didn't know it at the time. When they came in to tell us about you after the surgery, she passed out and fell flat on her face. Broke her nose." Al watched as Joe closed his eyes. "She fractured her cheekbone. The doctor took her for a C.T. scan and discovered she'd been shot. The bullet that went through you hit her. There wasn't any real damage; it was between the bones, and they took it out. But, well, she hasn't woken up yet. We arranged for her to be in here with you, hoping it would help her."

Slowly, Joe turned his head to look at her. His beautiful girl lay lifeless in the bed next to him. Her face was black and blue, and a heart monitor beeped with each beat of her heart. She was breathing on her own. Her mind was just in a slumber and there wasn't a fucking thing he could do to help her. He could barely pick up his hand.

Anger replaced his fear, and his heart rate kicked in, setting off alarms. The nurse came running into the room. "Mr. Blackshaw, you need to calm down." His tears rolled from his eyes. Another nurse came in. "I'm going to give you something to help you calm down and rest." She had a syringe in her hand, putting whatever was in it into Joe's I.V., and nearly instantly, his heart started to slow down. Soon, he was sleeping.

This went on for days. Every time he woke up, his tears would fall, and he would just get angry all over again, and every time they would give him something to sleep. In the big picture, he knew he needed to get fucking control. He hated being incapacitated like this. He needed to get stronger, not become an invalid. She needed him to take care of her, to help her wake up. They had a life to live. He needed her just as much as, if not more than, she needed him.

After a week, Joe learned to control his anger and was getting the shot less and less. He had been in the hospital for nearly three weeks now, and Roni still lay sleeping in the bed next to his.

One morning, Al and Becca came into the room. "Good to see you awake," Al said to him.

"Yeah, I'm on my way to get some x-rays so they can make sure I'm healed and I can get out of this fucking bed." His eyes moving to Roni.

"So I can hold my wife." His voice softened. "Al, why hasn't she woken up? They said, the longer she sleeps, the harder it will be to wake up. It's been weeks."

"I don't know, brother. She had been through so much before you met her. Maybe her body just needs to rest." But Al really didn't think that was the problem. He was there when she hit the floor. Although the C.T. scan showed no sign of a brain bleed, he just wasn't sure.

Two days later, Joe was released from the hospital, but he didn't leave. He wouldn't leave without her. He climbed in the bed with her, wrapping her in his embrace, and held her, his tears falling gently on her head. "Come on, beautiful. Wake up. I'm here," he whispered to her.

Days and days went by as he grew stronger and stronger. Becca came in one morning. "I heard one of the nurses say they are wanting to move Roni to a long-term care facility."

"Fuck that, she can come home with me."

"Joe, her mother wants her moved to a facility."

He laughed. "Her mother has no say."

"She is claiming that you are harmful to Roni and that you are the reason she is here. We aren't going to let Elizabeth anywhere near her."

"What about Mike? Did he survive all of this?"

"He is slow to recover. He's still in D.C., pissed that he can't be here with Roni. He's started divorce proceedings. He's done with Elizabeth."

Joe chuckled. But it was Roni who answered her. "It's about time."

Becca and Joe looked at her. His hand moved up to touch her face. "Did you just say that?"

She gently nodded. "What happened?"

"I'll get the nurse," Becca said.

"You've been asleep for a very long time. Open your eyes, baby, and let me see them."

~

The voices weren't familiar to her, but the subject of her mother was comforting, even though she hated her. There was someone in her bed holding her, and she didn't understand why. The voice said she had been asleep for a long time, but after searching her mind, she didn't know why.

She didn't want to open her eyes. She was terrified. Then she heard more voices.

"Could you please excuse us?"

"The doctor wants to examine her." That was the woman's voice from a few minutes ago.

Roni felt lips on her forehead. "I'll be right outside," the voice said softly.

As his weight lifted off the bed, she could hear people moving around the room. Opening her eyes, she caught a blurry glimpse of a man leaving her room and the door shutting.

"Hello, Veronica. My name is Dr. Hall. I've been taking care of you."

Her eyes blurry, she asked, "What happened to me? Why am I here?"

"You don't remember?" She slowly shook her head. "What is the last thing you remember?"

She searched her mind. "I remember walking into my apartment to find my fiancé having sex with another woman, and then I remember leaving."

"Was the man who left here your fiancé?"

"No, my fiancé is Tony Eden. I don't know who those people were. Has my father been here?"

The doctor looked at her, then at the nurse. "No, your father or mother haven't been here. Can you tell me your name?"

"Veronica Holloway. My father is Senator Michael Holloway. What is going on?"

"I'd like to do an exam first, and then we'll talk."

Fifteen minutes later, Roni asked him, "So, am I all right? When can I go home?"

"You've healed nicely. Your nose and cheek are fine."

"What happened to my nose?" She lifted her hand up to touch her nose.

Just then, the door opened and a huge man and a tiny woman walked in. "How is she, Doc? Can I take her home?"

Roni looked at the man. She was so taken aback by how beautiful he was that she forgot her voice. The tiny woman came over and took her hand. Roni snapped her head to look at her, pulling her hand away.

"Mr. Blackshaw, can I talk to you out in the hall?"

The man looked at her and smiled, and she felt her whole body warm. *What the fuck? Who the hell is he?* "I'll be right back."

Roni watched him walk out the door. "Hey." The woman was talking to her. "Are you all right? You look like you've seen a ghost."

Roni didn't say anything as she watched the man in the hallway through the glass. She had no idea who he was or who these people were. The nurse didn't leave her bedside the entire time. When the man turned his head to look at her, she felt her mouth go dry. She saw the pain in his eyes, which made her feel uncomfortable, so she turned her head.

Joe followed the doctor out into the hallway. "What's going on?"

"Mr. Blackshaw, I don't know how to say this, but your wife, well, she has no idea she is your wife. The last thing she remembers is witnessing her then fiancé having intercourse with someone else. After that it just goes blank for her."

"What?" Joe turned his head to look at her. She didn't remember him.

"It happens sometimes with a trauma such as this. She did hit her head pretty hard on the floor. When the mind cannot handle what has happened, it sometimes shuts off and refuses to remember. She was a mess when they brought you in here."

"How long will she be like this?" Joe asked, his eyes on Roni.

"There is no telling. You must be careful not to rush her memories.

I wasn't there, so I have no idea the trauma she suffered. If you tell her what happened, you could cause more damage. She said she was engaged to Tony Eden. Perhaps you could contact him? Maybe he would spark a memory."

"He's dead. He tried to kill her. That's who shot me."

"What about her parents?"

"Her father is still in recovery from being nearly murdered by Eden, and as far as I know, her mother isn't the type to care. She should be in jail for conspiracy to commit murder. Her life is a mess." His voice lowered. "Our life is a mess. Doc, how do I get her to come home with me? I need to tell her that she is my wife."

"Why don't we go in, and I will gently ask her questions. You just sit in the background. Let's see what she remembers."

"Okay."

When the door opened, Roni turned her head to see the doctor walk in. He leaned in and quietly asked Al and Becca to please leave the room. She watched as the beautiful man who was holding her sat in a chair across the room. His eyes stayed on her, watching her. She felt herself blush, and he smiled a small smile.

"Veronica?" the doctor asked.

Her eyes moved to him. "Roni, please. For some reason, I don't like Veronica."

He smiled at her. "Roni, would you tell me about your life?"

Crinkling her eyebrows, she tilted her head a fraction. "I don't understand."

"Tell me what your life is like."

She sat there looking at him and could feel the fear welling up inside of her. Fighting back tears, she said in the smallest of voices, "I don't think I'm very happy. My fiancé hurts me. Where is Tony? He should be here. No, wait, I remember leaving him. I caught him having sex with another woman in our apartment. That's all I can remember. Doctor, how long have I been here?"

"In this hospital, about a month."

Panic was taking over. "A month?" Her eyes skirted around the room before landing on the eyes of the man in the chair. "Who are you?" She nearly shouted, "Why do you keep looking at me?"

"My name is Joe Blackshaw. Your father hired me to watch out for you."

"My father? Why do you seem so familiar to me?"

She watched as his eyes moved to the doctor, who nodded to him. "I've been with you for nearly six months."

Roni's breath hitched in her chest. "Six months?" She looked back to the doctor as a tear slipped down her cheek. "I can't remember the last six months of my life?"

"It would seem so. Roni, you took a pretty big fall when you passed out a month ago. That's when you broke your nose and cracked your cheekbone. You suffered quite a traumatic experience right before. When things like that happen, the brain shuts off and represses those traumatic memories. Gradually, they will come back. Well, at least, that's been my experience."

"You mean they might never come back to me?" Her eyes moved to the beautiful man sitting in the chair. "Why were you in bed with me? Who are you to me?"

His eyes moved to the doctor again. Roni watched the doctor just barely shake his head before the man turned back to Roni. "Why don't you just let this happen naturally? If your mind short circuits again, you may lose more of your memories, or even…"

"Or even what?" She could feel the panic growing again.

"You could slip back into a coma if your mind overloads, if we give you too much too soon." He reached out to squeeze her hand. "Just let it happen naturally. I'm going to release you today, and Joe can take you home."

Her eyes shifted to the beautiful man in the chair. The doctor and the nurse left the room, leaving the two of them alone. Her mouth had gone dry from his stare. "I'm not going to hurt you." His voice was kind and gentle. "You don't need to be afraid of me."

"I'm not. As least, not like you think."

His smile was huge. "What does that mean?"

Roni grew warm in places she hadn't felt in a very long time, if ever. She shook her head. "Nothing. Do I have clothes?"

Just then, the door opened, and the tiny woman and huge man from before came back in. "I brought some clothes over that you left in the loft." She bent down and picked up a bag then handed it to Roni.

"I'm sorry, but who are you?" Roni questioned.

Becca smiled at her. "Becca Blackshaw, and this is my husband Al. He and Joe are brothers. They've been protecting you."

"Yes, protecting me." She looked inside the bag. "Thank you." She pulled back the covers and slid out of the bed, nearly falling on her wobbly legs. Joe made it to her in two long strides, wrapping his arm around her waist and pulling her to him.

"I got you." His breath was warm on her head. "Let me help you." He walked slowly with her to the bathroom and then inside.

She stood there looking at him. "Would you excuse me?"

Chuckling, he backed out of the room. "Becca, would you mind helping her." He kept his eyes on her green ones. "We can't have you falling down and hurting that beautiful head of yours."

She smirked at him as Becca came in.

Joe backed out of the room, closing the door behind him, keeping his hands on the frame as he hung his head and tears spilled from his eyes. He could hear Becca talking gently to her. Al walked up to him and put his arm around his shoulders.

"She'll remember. Give her time. She's been through a great deal. You didn't see her when she thought you were dead. She was like a zombie. Come on, brother." Al turned him away from the door.

"I have never loved another human being like I love her. What if she never remembers me?"

Al smiled at him. "Then make her fall in love with you again. Listen, you both have a second chance, only this time you don't have a fucking madman chasing you. You can do this right now, instead of with all the fear. Let her see the man she loves so deeply."

Joe chuckled as he wiped his face. "Since when did you become so sappy?"

Al busted out laughing. "You've met my wife, right? Who knew the love of a good woman could bring either of us to our knees? The woman in there does just that. One look, Joe. She just has to give me one look, and I would give her the fucking moon." He lowered his voice. "There is nothing wrong with admitting that's how you feel. Let it go, Joe. Let yourself be free from the bonds this fucking life we've lived has placed on you. It's a wonderful feeling."

As Joe nodded, the bathroom door opened and the girls walked out. Joe turned to look at Roni, seeing the confusion in her eyes. Tilting her head, she looked into his soul. Smiling, he asked as he moved toward her, "Will you come back to the loft with us? There is plenty of room there."

"Why wouldn't I go home to my parents' house?"

Joe swallowed and took a deep breath. "The reason you have no memory happened there. The doctor thought it best that you gain your memory back before you go there."

"But my parents are there."

Becca walked up to her, putting her hand on her back. "No, Roni, they're not. Your father is still in D.C., and your mother hasn't been a positive in your life. You would be there alone, and it's not a good idea for you to be alone right now. Al and I are going to stay at the loft with you."

Roni looked at Joe. "And I suppose you will be there as well?"

"I would like to stay there, but if you aren't comfortable with that, I can stay at my place."

~

The doctor walked in before she had a chance to answer. "I have your discharge papers. I've included the number of a doctor who might be able to help you with your memories if you want to call her. She's very good."

"Thank you." Roni took the papers from him then looked at Joe. "I'd like to go now. Will you take me?"

The conversation she and Becca had in the bathroom left her with a great deal to think about. Becca had told her how much Joe loved her, and that they were a couple. But it was all right that she didn't remember that. Becca had told her that she would stay at the loft as long as Roni needed her to and that she understood how scared she was. Then she briefly told her about how she felt when her husband and children died, and how lost she felt, and explained how Joe helped her find her peace of mind.

Roni needed to trust something, anything. Her memories of Tony were so fresh in her mind. He was not a nice man, and well, this Joe person made her feel safe. He was freaking huge, and Becca's husband, Al, was just as big.

As they drove to the loft, Joe kept his eyes on her. It made her feel uncomfortable, yet safe all at the same time. When she turned her head to look at him, though his smile was soft, she could see pain and fear in his eyes. She forced a small smile before turning her head as they pulled into the garage.

Al got out and opened her door. She hesitated as Joe got out and opened Becca's door. Al smiled. "It'll be fine. You will have your own room."

"I'm just not sure this is the place for me to be."

Joe had walked around the car. "Could you excuse us for a few minutes?" Al nodded and walked away. Standing by the door, Roni had to stop herself from touching him. He was beautiful, and she felt so drawn to him.

She looked up at him. "Who are you to me?"

He forced a smile to his lips. "It's not important right now. I can't tell you anything really, but just know that I will never hurt you, and I will be here if you need me for anything."

"Do you love me, Joe Blackshaw?" She said his name and it felt right to say it. No matter what his words were, she could see in his eyes that he did. It didn't make any sense to her that she couldn't remember this man in front of her.

His smile was slow and soft. "With all that I am." His voice was gentle, his hand coming up to touch her cheek. "With all that I am. Come on, I'm sure you are hungry."

When he touched her, she felt her body's natural inclination to lean into him, but she didn't know him. Not like she believed he knew her. Nodding, she got out of the car and followed them into the elevator.

Joe nearly had a heart attack when she asked him if he loved her. The doctor told him not to give her any information, to let her figure it out on her own. But he would never deny her the words or the knowledge of his feelings for her. She was his great love, and no matter how much time it took, he was going to do what Al told him to do. He was going to make her fall in love with him all over again.

Their life was their own now. No more running and certainly no more fear of anything. Mike would just have to understand how he felt about her and know that he would give his own life for her.

He led her to the room they'd shared before. "This is your room now. Your things are in the closet. The bathroom is here." He walked over and opened the bathroom door. "I know you like Chinese food, so I'll go call in an order. It'll take about twenty minutes to get here." He moved to the door, to where she was, stopping in front of her.

It was difficult at best for him not to wrap her in his arms when she turned her head up to look at him with her emerald green eyes. "Thank you."

Smiling, he gave her a bit of a chuckle. "Anything, anytime. I'll leave you be. I'm sure you want to take a shower. All of your things are still in the bathroom."

He went to move around her when she put her hand on his chest, stopping him in his tracks. "You're very familiar with me." Her voice was quiet. "I'm terrified that I don't know you. I'm more terrified that you know me so well."

"I'm sorry this has happened to you. I am not going to hurt you, and I am not going to impose myself. Time is what the doc said. I'm a very patient man." His fingers trailed along her jaw. "Hopefully, you'll remember who I am, who I am to you. I'll be in the living room."

Leaving the bedroom was the hardest thing he had ever done. He wanted to hold her, to love her, but he couldn't. He stood in the hallway trying to catch his breath, trying to gain some sort of control over his overwhelming desire to scream.

Roni stood there as he silently closed the door. She felt the tears fall on her cheeks but had no idea why she was crying. He was so beautiful, and she was pissed she didn't remember him. He'd said he loved her. Did she love him in return? She thought she would be a fool not to love him. Shaking her head and smiling, she decided to go take a shower.

After stripping out of her clothes, she stood under the hot water for what seemed like forever. As she washed, flashes of memory came —hands on her body, teeth gently biting her shoulder and neck. She tried to get them out by shaking her head. She quickly washed her hair and got out. Standing, looking at the shower, she couldn't form an entire moment, just the flashes of memory. Were they even her memories or just a fantasy?

As she dried off, she happened to see her shoulder in the mirror and froze. Turning, she saw the scar. She didn't remember a scar like this. Her fingers touched the small indented circle. "What the fuck?" Quickly, she dried off and dressed. When she opened her door, Joe was there. "I was just going to knock. Food is here. You hungry?"

"I could eat," she smarted, which drew a smile from him. She wanted to ask him if he knew about the scar on her shoulder, but she thought it should wait.

~

The four of them ate without much conversation. Joe had to stop himself from staring at her. He didn't want her to feel uncomfortable. When she finished eating, she excused herself and went back to her room. Sitting in the middle of the bed, she tried to remember him, to remember them. They seemed to know her, but they were being very careful with her.

What happened to me? What was so horrific that I blocked it from my memory?

So many questions she had. Lying on the bed, she pulled a pillow under her head and closed her eyes, trying to force them. There was a knock on the door, and she was sure it was him. "Come in." Her voice didn't sound like her own.

"You okay?" She was right; it was him.

Sitting up, she looked at him. "I'm not sure."

"Can I come in? Maybe I can help you."

Nodding, she watched him walk in and close the door. He sat in the chair across from the bed. Her eyes never left his. They sat in silence for a few minutes. "When I was in the shower…" She paused, licking her lips. "I had; I don't know… thoughts maybe I mean, I don't know if they are memories or not."

"Do you want to tell me?"

She felt herself blush. "Well, as I washed, it was like there were other hands on me." Joe smiled at her. "Then… I don't know… I felt gentle bites on my neck and shoulder. Almost as if a ghost was touching me." She watched as his pupils dilated. "So, would you know anything about that?" He didn't say anything, just nodded. "Would you be willing to fill in the blanks?" Her whole body was pink with the flush of blush moving through her. "Was it you?"

"Yes," he said softly.

"Oh." She paused, her eyes locked with his. "I think I'm tired."

Joe stood. "I'll be on the couch if you need me." He smiled at her.

"Would you stay in here with me? I'm a bit more than freaked out. Maybe watch over me?"

Sitting back down with his arms on his knees, he smiled. "Anything, anytime. Why don't you change? I'll stay here for as long as you need me."

~

Joe realized when he stood to leave that he was shaking. Sitting there watching her struggle to ask him to stay made him uncomfortable. She was his wife. She should never feel that way.

"I'm sorry, I have no right to ask you. You don't need to stay here."

He watched as a tear fell on her cheek. He was moving, kneeling on the floor in front of her. "You have every right. I don't want to leave you alone. I don't want to go. I want to stay, but I didn't want to make you uncomfortable." She nodded as another tear fell. "May I?" His hand moved to her face. He wrapped it around her neck, his thumb wiping the tears. "Don't cry, beautiful. Everything is going to be all right. We'll get through this."

When she licked her lips, he had to keep his moan silent. She whispered. "Why don't I remember anything? Why don't I remember you?"

"You will. Things you do will trigger the memories. It'll come back."

"Like in the shower? I was in the shower with you?"

"Yes. We were in the shower. Why don't you go on and change? I'll be right here when you come back."

He watched as she climbed off the bed. When the closet door closed, he dropped his head. "Fuck." He was struggling to not tell her that she was his wife. He was struggling to not touch her. When the door opened, he lifted his head. She was standing in the doorway with a tiny pair of shorts covering her perfectly plump ass and a nearly see-through t-shirt doing a poor job of masking her breasts. His cock grew hard under the denim of his jeans. If he stood, he was sure she would see him. Turning his body away from her, he pulled back the covers. "Come on. Get in."

As she walked to the bed, he could see her breasts sway with each step. When she climbed in, he got a view of her perfect ass. His hand came very close to caressing it, but he stopped himself.

After covering her with the blanket, he ran his finger along her jaw. "Good night, beautiful." She gave him a soft smile as he stood and turned his body away from her.

"You're not sleeping here?"

Joe chuckled. "No, sweetheart." His voice came out a bit firmer than he wanted. "I'll be in the chair."

"But… I thought…"

Joe sat and leaned forward, looking at her with his hands on his knees. "It wouldn't be right for me to sleep in that bed with you right now."

Her eyes bore into his. He was struggling. This had to be the hardest thing he had ever done. Not touching her, not holding her. God, he wanted to kiss her. He tried to convey that in his look. Her eyes hardened, and his heart sped up. She was getting angry; he knew this look. He nearly chuckled, but he didn't want to upset her. He loved the range of emotions she revealed through her eyes. His heart was full. He couldn't wait to spend his life finding each and every one of them. He wanted to be his cocky self, but he couldn't confuse her any more than she already was.

Instead of saying anything in return, she just rolled over, away from him. Joe sat back in the chair, his eyes scanning the outline of her body, the deep curve from her waist to that luscious ass of hers. His cock was painfully stiff, pressing against the denim. With all that he was, he wanted to fuck her hard.

"Why do you stare at me, Joe Blackshaw?"

This time, he did chuckle, because she asked him that more than a few times. "Because you are so damn beautiful." His voice sounded gravelly from the blazing desire coursing through him.

She laughed, but it was more like a smart-assed laugh and brought him to his feet. He moved silently to the side of the bed, his hand moving on its own to touch her hair.

"Because you are so damn beautiful," he whispered.

Roni turned at her waist, her ample breasts halfway falling out of her t-shirt, to look at him. His eyes moved to look at her. "Like something you see?" She was baiting him.

"Everything I see, I like. It's not just one thing." His fingers trailed along the rise of her nearly exposed breast. He watched as her glorious nipple hardened. As he pulled his hand away, he trailed his baby finger along her nipple.

"Then why are you sleeping in the chair?" Licking her lips, she pulled her bottom lip between her teeth.

Smiling, Joe reached to pull her lip loose. "You aren't whole, and it would be wrong to climb in this bed with you. Not until you remember who I am to you."

"What if I don't ever remember?"

He smiled. "That nipple right there tells me you will. Goodnight, beautiful." After running his finger along her jaw, he turned and went back to the chair, leaving her to watch him walk away. When he sat and turned, she had rolled over. He dropped his head back against the chair and closed his eyes. As tired as he was, he just couldn't seem to shut off his mind. A drink would be helpful, so he waited for her to fall asleep.

Al was sitting in the dark when he made his way out into the living room. "You all right?"

"No." Joe sighed. "I think I need a drink. I think I know how you felt when you and Becca were separated in the beginning. I'm not sure I am going to be able to get through this without touching her, kissing her."

"Just remember, brother, she is broken right now. She needs to find her way back to you."

"Yeah, I know, but that is easier said than done." He poured himself a drink and sat in the chair across from Al. "Why are you out here and not in there wrapped around your wife?"

"I was talking to Mom. We need to bury our brothers' ashes. Mom wants us to come home as soon as we can. She wants to put them next to Ali."

Joe leaned forward, putting his arms on his knees, and dropped his head. "I still can't believe that fucker killed them."

"Me neither, and I can't tell you how fucking fantastic it felt to empty my clip into that fucker. As far as I'm concerned, it wasn't enough. I wanted to beat that bastard with my fist. I wanted to watch his eyes as he realized he was fucking dead."

"I hear you."

Just as the words came out of his mouth, a scream filled the comfortable silence and had both of them rushing through the loft. Joe was first through the door, to find Roni sitting up hysterical. Her eyes shot up to look at them.

"Oh my God. Oh my God." She sobbed.

He was across the room, crawling up the bed before she could say another word. He pulled her into his arms. "I got you, beautiful. I got you."

Al smiled and backed out of the room, pulling the door closed. Becca was standing in the hall. "I think she just remembered what happened," he said softly. Taking her hand, he led her back to their bedroom, with the hope that all was going to be right in their world again.

The flashes came and came again. There wasn't a clear picture, just fragments of things. Her heart slammed in her chest when the loud pops echoed in her mind. She couldn't place them. Were they fireworks? Nothing was clear, just noises, echoes of a life she couldn't remember.

Her body thrashed in the bed as she struggled to breathe. It was as if she was suffocating. In her mind, the flashes were brief, the booms loud. Eleven booms fired off over and over as if a record was skipping. The sound, the vibration haunted her, causing her to scream as she tried to make it stop. Her hands over her ears, her body sat up, and her scream sounded out, snapping her out of her sleep, out of the nightmare that haunted her.

Before she knew what was happening, she felt a familiar, warm embrace that not only calmed her but completely surrounded her in a cocoon of safety. Her hands grabbed him, pulling herself to his warmth.

"I got you, beautiful. I got you."

For some reason, those words gave her the greatest comfort. Her breath came in hard puffs of air as she calmed down. Her body was shaking, her heart slamming in her chest, but it all seemed to slow as his warmth filled her. Who was this man to her, that she felt so safe with him?

"Who are you?" she stuttered out in puffs of air. "Who are you?"

He didn't say anything, but she felt his hold tighten around her. They sat in the middle of the bed for a long time. When she finally calmed down, she slowly pulled away from him and looked at his face. His cheeks were wet, so she moved her hands up from his sides to gently wipe his face. "Who are we to each other, Joe Blackshaw?"

He smiled at her, but for whatever reason, she knew it wasn't real. "You'll remember who we are to each other. I can't tell you. I can't change the healing of your mind. It could damage you even more. The doctor told me that, if we flood your mind with your life, you could fall back into a coma and run the risk of you never remembering. You have to do this on your own. You want to talk about what happened?"

"It felt like I was being suffocated. I couldn't breathe. Then loud pops, like booms, over and over. One, then two, then one, then like eight or nine more. The pattern just continued over and over, getting louder and louder each time. I couldn't breathe. It wouldn't stop. One, then two, then one, then a whole line of booms." She felt his fingers press into her back as he pulled her into his chest again.

"God, beautiful. I am so sorry this is happening to you."

"Joe," she whispered into his chest, her hand fisting into his shirt. "I have a scar on my shoulder that wasn't there before. I don't know what happened to me, and that terrifies me more than anything Tony has done to me."

His hand moved on its own to her scar. It was still very pink. When his fingers gently brushed over it, she recoiled against him.

"Do you know what happened to me?"

Dropping his head to her shoulder, his lips pressed against the skin as he nodded.

"Tell me."

He lifted his head to her ear. "I can't, beautiful. You need to let it all come back to you."

"Will you stay with me?" Pulling back, she looked deep into his eyes. "I don't want to be alone."

"I told you I wasn't going anywhere."

Her heart raced. She wanted this beautiful stranger, who wasn't really a stranger; at least, she didn't think he was. She wanted him to sleep in the bed with her, but she didn't know how to ask him. So, she just nodded. Pulling away from him and getting off his lap, she got back under the covers while he climbed off the big bed.

Joe had never felt such distress before. She needed him more than he could imagine, and he had to deny her again and again. He was a wreck, an emotional wreck. When she was comfortable, Joe reached down, touching her cheek. Looking into her eyes, he could see fear, and it tore him to shreds.

"I'm so sorry." His voice was soft and gentle as his fingertips touched her lips. Turning, he walked to the chair and sat. She was lying on her side watching him, looking at him. He didn't move. He tried with all that he was to convey his love for her in his eyes.

With each blink of her eyes, they stayed closed longer and longer. Eventually, they stayed closed and she fell asleep. Slowly, he put his head back and closed his eyes, and sleep took him.

When his eyes opened again, it was light out. Picking his head up, he looked at the bed, but it was empty. He felt panic rise in his chest. Turning his head, he saw the door open and then heard voices. Calming down, he got up and grabbed some clean clothes, and headed to the shower.

Standing under the hot water felt good. He hadn't had a decent shower in a long time. His thoughts wandered to her, on the life he'd led for twenty years. None of the life he'd led before meant a fucking thing now that he found her, found the rest of his life. He could feel the tears well up in his eyes at what was nearly lost six weeks ago. With his hands on the wall of the shower, he let it all go. Every fear he had felt since meeting her, how they all nearly lost their lives to that fucking madman. Losing his brothers. None of it made any sense. None of it was what he'd planned for his life. Hell, love was the furthest thing from his mind when he met her. But wasn't that how love came? Hard and fast, just like the bullet that nearly ended him. After gaining some semblance of control, he washed and then stepped out, grabbing a towel. His back to the door, he felt her before he heard her.

"Uh."

Joe froze, feeling her move toward him, then he felt her fingers as she touched the scars on his shoulder and back. "Roni." His voice sounded strangled with the anger he was working on compressing and the raging desire he felt for her.

"The booms," she whispered. "They were gunshots." He could feel her fingers tremble as she touched him. "You were shot. I was shot. Who did this, Joe? Who shot us?"

Wrapping the towel around him, his cock harder than stone, he half-turned. "Let me get dressed and we'll talk about this."

Her hand trailed down his back as she moved out of the bathroom. Joe watched her, her eyes not leaving him. When she disappeared from his sight, he grabbed his jeans. After pulling them on, he grabbed his t-shirt and pulled it over his head as he walked into the bedroom to find her sitting on the bed.

He knelt in front of her. "How'd you sleep?"

"Really good."

"No more dreams?"

She shook her head. "They weren't dreams, were they? They were memories."

"No, they weren't dreams."

"Who shot us?"

"I was the one who was shot. The bullet passed through me," he moved his shirt to show her the exit wound, "and hit you in the shoulder."

"You were in front of me? Why?"

"I was protecting you." His voice sounded strained. He knew he was giving her too much information, but he couldn't deny her the truth.

"You took a bullet for me? Joe, please tell me who you are to me, that you would take a bullet for me."

Reaching up, he touched her face. "Baby steps, beautiful. Baby steps."

She reached up to touch his face. "You are so beautiful. I can't imagine you being so important to me, or me so important to you. I'm not..." Her head lowered, and her hand dropped.

"Hey, you are," he whispered. "You so are."

He watched as her head slowly rose, their eyes connecting, and he saw it. He saw the love she had for him. He saw the fear, the desire swirling in her green eyes. She nodded slightly. "Becca made breakfast if you're hungry."

With a smile, he told her, "I could eat," which drew a small giggle from her. Joe stood. "After you." He put his hand out for her to walk in front of him. He wanted to look at her beautiful full ass. An ass he missed, an ass he couldn't wait to taste again.

After they ate, Roni and Becca were cleaning up. "This is a nice place. How long have you and Al lived here?"

Becca laughed. "We don't live here. This was Al's place when we met. We live in a cabin on a lake in upper Idaho. I actually miss the place. I don't care so much for the city."

Roni looked at her. "Then why are you here?"

Bec put her hand on Roni's arm. "We are here for you. Al can't leave until you are whole. Until Joe is whole."

"What if I'm never whole? What if I don't get my memory back?"

"I have faith that you will," Joe said from the dining room. "Baby steps, remember?"

Roni turned. "You're so sure of that. You can't be sure of anything." Her voice became hard. "I've lost six months of my life. These people have put their lives on hold. Hell, you've put your life on hold, and for what? To babysit me? I can't let you do that. All of you need to just go on with your lives, and I need to go home. I need to see my father and settle this with Tony. I can't marry him."

Joe looked at Al then back to Roni who was visibly upset. "Listen," he began, but she jumped him.

"No. No, I'm not going to listen. You can't tell me what to do. God knows that fucker has been controlling me for the past year. I'm not afraid of him anymore. My father is a goddamn senator. He will protect me." She went to walk away, and Joe grabbed her arm.

"No, sweetheart. You…" He stopped when she froze. He watched as all the life drained out of her eyes.

His words passed through her ears and shot through her brain like an arrow ripping it open. Flashes began like lit fireworks. With each boom, each flash of light, her body jumped involuntarily. The woods, the creek, the heavenly smell of the shadow in front of her, all caused her to jump away. She didn't feel scared, not like she should have. She felt excited.

Joe stood stock still, and Al was frozen as they watched her body twitch. Looking at Al, he slightly shook his head, indicating for Joe not to move.

The smell of sweat filled her nose, the glorious feeling of freedom as her body became overwhelmed with emotion. What was she doing? What the fuck was happening? Her mind swirled like a whirlpool. She heard her voice as she screamed. She felt her hands grab her head as the flashes continued. She was in the woods again, alone, and it was dark. Flash after flash.

Searing pain crossed her cheek as cold raced down her back. The tears fell from her eyes as she felt relief, satisfaction, and an overwhelming sense of protection. Then everything went black.

Joe watched as she pulled her hair, screamed, and then cried. It was when her legs buckled, and she started falling, that he moved, catching her limp body. Grabbing her in his arms, he looked at Al.

"What the fuck just happened?"

"I think she just had a memory. What the fuck? I'm going to call the doctor. Maybe he can help." Al reached for his phone.

"Come on, let's get her in bed." Becca put her hand on Joe's arm. "This is good. She's remembering." She led Joe into the bedroom where he laid her on the bed. Becca went into the bathroom, grabbing a cool washcloth to put on her head.

Joe was physically shaken by what he had just witnessed. Sitting in the chair, he put his head in his hands. He was struggling to breathe. She was so distressed. Their life wasn't supposed to be like this. Looking up, he could see her lifeless body. With all that he was, he fought with himself not to go over and crawl in bed with her and hold her. He knew she was going to be scared when she woke up. If she woke up.

Al walked in. "The doc said what happened is normal with memory recovery. He said she should be fine physically. Mentally, he said to call him if anything has changed."

"What if she doesn't fucking wake up?"

"Then we take her in. Calm down. You need to be strong for her. She'll wake up."

For hours, Joe sat there looking at her. Becca and Al had gone to bed. He couldn't stand not being next to her. Slowly, he walked to the bed. After climbing in, he drew her into his arms and pulled her to his chest, wrapping her in his warmth. The tears came, he couldn't stop them. He didn't want to stop them. He hated knowing what she must be going through. So much torture she'd endured from that fucking asshole.

Eventually, he fell asleep in the only place he ever wanted to be. Next to her, with her in his arms.

CHAPTER TWELVE

Roni started to come back, and she felt so safe, so warm. She felt loved. Her eyes opened to a darkened room, hearing a steady heartbeat in her ear. Breathing in, she knew that scent. It was him. A strange calm came over her as her memories came flooding back to her. The love she felt for him. The love he felt for her. His tender touches. His beautiful, sometimes rough words and his love. Her husband. He was her husband.

From deep within her, she felt a blossoming of warmth, an overwhelming joy that he was alive and had her in his embrace, where she belonged. Where she would always belong. Moving her hands up his chest, she pushed back to look at him.

With his eyes still closed, her fingers touched his perfect lips, the lips that kissed her, loved her. They trailed along his eyes, the eyes that could see into her soul. The creases along his temple, the touch of grey in his hair. Down his stoic jawline. "So beautiful," she whispered as her fingers trailed along his lips again. Leaning in, she softly kissed them.

He moved his hand up her back, into her hair. Wrapping it around the base of her neck, he deepened the kiss, taking her breath away. He was all she ever wanted in life. Just the thought that Tony almost took him from her was more than she could handle.

"My husband." She smiled as he froze. "Thank you for surviving. God, Joe, I was so scared. I thought I was never going to have this again."

"Aww, beautiful, I'm not going anywhere." His mouth crashed down on hers.

When they finally pulled away from one another, she smiled at him. "I'm sorry."

He shook his head. "You have nothing to be sorry for. So, you remember?"

"Everything. What happened to my mother? I need to go see my father. We need to tell him that we are married. I want our life now. I want to lay in bed with you all day and make love. I want everything, Joe. Can I have everything with you?" She teased him.

"Anything, anytime, anywhere." He pulled her on top of him.

Roni let herself feel him. She let herself not care about anything but him, them. She remembered everything. "Joe, I love you."

"Mmm, I've waited so long to hear you say that." Deepening the kiss, he rolled her onto her side. "Roni." His voice was gravelly from the lust roaring through his veins.

"Please, Joe." She pulled his shirt up his back and over his head.

Smiling at her, his hands moved up, ripping her shirt off her body. When Joe unclasped her bra and released her gloriously plump breasts, he moaned. His hand cupped one then his mouth engulfed her nipple.

She arched her back at the sensation, feeling his cock on her hip. Her hands moved on their own to unbutton his jeans, releasing him into her hands. She pumped his cock, gripping him tightly. His hips jerked with each pump. Roni felt his teeth bite down around her nipple as he released in her hand. Joe moved down her stomach, undoing her jeans. Pushing up, he pulled them off along with her panties. After handing them to her so she could wipe her hands, he slowly opened her legs. Roni dropped the jeans as her back came off the bed. She knew what was coming.

Joe sat back on his heels to look at her. "So fucking sweet," he moaned, smiling at her he leaned down and took all that she had to give him. With gentle swipes of his tongue, his taste buds came alive. She was his ambrosia, his very own nectar. She grabbed his head as her third orgasm blew through her, her fingernails pressing into his skull, making him fully hard again.

He wasn't sure how his jeans got off, but when he slowly pushed inside of her, she sank her teeth into his shoulder to stop herself from crying out. They made love for a long time, so slow, so tender. He had never wanted a woman like this, no one but her. Her silken walls surrounded him, her velvet cocoon taking him to the place he never thought he would see. Heaven. They came together, wrapped in each other's arms, their mouths connected in a passion that would set the city on fire.

He felt so complete, so connected to the woman in his arms. She was his, and he was hers. Nothing else in the world mattered as long as he had her. Holding on, they parted, and he smiled at her. "Welcome home, wife."

Roni giggled at him. "It's good to be home, husband."

Tucking her into his side, with his leg draped over her hip and her leg slipped between his, they fell asleep.

Joe heard the door gently close. Opening his eyes, he saw it was light out and he was naked with Roni in his arms. Smiling, he hoped last night wasn't a dream. His fingers needed to touch her. As he trailed them down her side, she giggled, picking her head up. Joe pulled her on top of him then held her face with both hands.

"I hoped it wasn't a dream," he whispered in her mouth as they kissed.

He felt her move down his body. She was soaked with his juices. Walking up his chest, she slid him inside her and based him with a deep guttural moan. It was probably the most beautiful thing to watch her rock back and forth, her breasts swaying for him like the flowers in a field touched by a sweet breeze. He was mesmerized watching her enjoy herself. The feeling of her swollen bud rubbing on him was going to be the end of him.

"Joe, does this feel like a dream?" Her words were filled with lust as she moved a bit faster, pushing down a bit harder. "Ah, God." He pushed up as she pushed back, covering her body with goose flesh.

"Ah, beautiful. I'm going to come."

"Me... too..."

He felt her body clamp around his cock and then cover it with her cum, sending him over the edge. Pulse after pulse, he filled her. She didn't stop moving until every drop was released. Then she gently lay on his chest.

Joe felt the tears as they slowly slid down his face. His arms wrapped around her. "I was so scared," he whispered. "So fucking scared you wouldn't remember us, this, me."

Picking her head up, she saw his tears and moved up his body to look into his eyes. "When I woke up in the hospital, I wasn't afraid. Not like I should have been. What I felt was safe, loved, and warm. I could feel you then. I don't think my love for you ever left me. I've never been loved like this, Joe. Never." Her fingers trailed along his lips. "You're in my heart, embedded in my soul. You're mine, Joe Blackshaw, and I plan on keeping you."

"Sweetheart, there has never been a woman who has captured me the way you have. I have never cried while a woman made love to me. Hell, you are the only one who has done it. I'm not going anywhere, ever. You're stuck with me."

She giggled, and his heart exploded. "That's a good thing."

"As much as I want to stay here all day, we've already had a visitor. So, why don't we take a shower and clean up this bed? I love the smell of us, but I'm not so sure Al and Becca would appreciate it."

Roni giggled as she rolled off him. "I'm sure they wouldn't either." She grabbed his hand. "Come, husband, and wash me."

Joe didn't argue, he was right behind her. She was even more glorious wet. When they finished, they stripped the bed then remade it. Joe took the sheets and started the laundry while Roni made her way to the kitchen, where Becca was cooking.

"Good morning, Becca."

Bec smiled at her. "Should I be scolding Joe when he comes out here?"

She shook her head. "It's all good."

Joe came around the corner and laughed. "She remembers everything."

Al came in from the balcony. "Mom wants us in Chicago as soon as possible. She wants to put the boys to rest. Then Becca and I are going home. I miss my quiet." Looking at Roni, he smiled. "Damn glad to see you're back. Now, maybe this guy will calm the fuck down."

Everyone laughed. "Come on, I've made breakfast." Becca motioned everyone to the table.

After they ate, Joe flipped the laundry and headed to the bedroom. "We should pack everything up and take it with us."

Roni smiled at him. "Are we going back to the islands? I'd like to go back there."

"We are, indeed, but to Chicago first and then to see your dad. I need to tell him that we are married."

She giggled at him. "He isn't going to be happy. You know that, right?"

"I know, but I'm hoping he knows I'm a good man who will give you a good life."

"Will you?" she smarted.

He slinked toward her with a Cheshire grin on his face. "Better than good." His arms wrapped around her waist, pulling her to him. Roni wrapped her arms around his neck, pushing up on her tippy toes. Joe grabbed her, pulling her up, her legs wrapping around his waist. Joe moved to the wall, pressing her against it, kissing her deeply. "So much better than good."

"Well, if this is how you are going to demonstrate that to my father, you might want to rethink it." She busted out in a fit of giggles.

"If there wasn't a plane waiting for us, I would fuck you into next week," he whispered on her lips.

Breathless, she whispered on his lips, "Well, there's a bed on that plane."

He chuckled. "No way, darling. Not with my brother on the other side of the door." Joe smacked her on the ass. "Come on, let's get out of here. The sooner we get all this done, the sooner we can have our life back."

He let her go, kissing her one last time. "You know Christmas has come and gone, right? Our first Christmas as a married couple, and we spent it in comas."

"I know, but we will have a Christmas. I promise."

She turned to look at him. "So sure of yourself, Mr. Blackshaw."

"Always, Mrs. Blackshaw."

They packed and met Becca, Al, Ella, and Mr. Fluff in the living room. Everyone was ready. They loaded into the SUV and headed to the airport.

~

The flight was silent. Roni could feel the tension coming from Joe. As she looked around the plane, she couldn't help but notice Becca looking at her. She gave her a small smile. Joe and Al were going to bury their brothers. She couldn't even begin to imagine she knew what they were feeling. Having buried their sister as well, she felt for them. She felt for her new mother in law.

Not having any real experience in handling sorrow, she decided to just be his partner, be his wife. Be the best she could be for him, simply because he had done exactly the same for her. Reaching over, she took his hand in hers. He turned his head to look at her. "I love you," she whispered.

"I love you."

When they landed, they headed to the private hanger and loaded into another SUV to drive to his mother's. Roni looked out the window most of the way. As the city disappeared and the suburbs came into view, Joe moved over next to her, pulling her close to his chest.

"I just want to let you know that this isn't going to be easy, and I apologize now if it feels as if I'm pulling away from you. I'm new to this sharing of feelings, and there are feelings I'm not sure I can handle," he said into her neck as he kissed it softly.

Turning, she wrapped her arms around his neck, pulling herself up onto his lap. "I understand. Just know that I am right here. I am not going to freak out on you. I love you. Please don't forget that."

He sweetly kissed her. "I won't."

Roni felt the car slow. Turning her head, she looked out the window as the car came to a stop in the driveway.

"I love you, beautiful," Joe said to her.

Roni ran her hands through his hair. Grabbing hold of it and pulling his head back, she leveled him with her kiss. "I love you, husband." After climbing off him, she turned to see his smile. They climbed out of the car and headed up to the house.

Sally met them at the door, hugging each of them. "Al, Becca, you can bunk in Al's old room, and Joey and Roni, you can sleep in your room."

"Thanks, Mom," Joe said, hugging her.

"I've got dinner in the oven, and Pastor Brad is coming over to talk about the service tomorrow. I would like to put my boys to rest."

Roni could hear the sadness in her voice. "I'm so sorry, Sally."

"This is not your fault, dear. It was their job. Why don't you all go up and freshen up? We want to look nice for Pastor Brad." She left them in the front hall.

Al shrugged his shoulders at Joe, who looked at Alex. "I think she has a thing for Pastor Brad," he said to Joe.

Laughing and shaking his head, he took Roni's hand and led her upstairs. When the door closed, he grabbed her, wrapping her in his arms. "I need my wife," he moaned against her neck.

"I'm right here. Not going anywhere." He picked her up, moving them to the bed. Laying her down, Joe began to ravish her, but Roni wasn't having it. "Joe." He picked his head up, popping her nipple out of his mouth. Her hand touched his face. "Not here. Please not here. I can't do this in your mother's home."

He smiled. “My mother raised five boys. Trust me, she knows what goes on up here.”

She still refused him. “No. I respect her, and that means not having sex in her home. I can’t do this. Not here. Not now.”

She went to get up, but Joe put his hand on her stomach. “Hey, what’s going on?” She shook her head. Moving his hand, she got off the bed. “Roni, talk to me.” Joe sat up.

He watched as she spun around. His heart jumped at the fire in her eyes. God, he loved the expressions in this woman’s eyes. His smile was huge. “We are here to bury your brothers and are staying in your mother’s home. I am better than this. I am not some self-centered stuck up society bitch who thinks the rules of life don’t apply to me.”

Joe was off the bed. He knew he’d startled her when she backed away from him. He didn’t give her time to react when he grabbed her up in his arms, moving across the room, and hitting the wall a bit harder than he intended. His hands moved to her face. “Those were words I spit out of my mouth that were never intended to do anything but hurt you. I can never take them back. But never once did I think or feel that you were that person. Right now, I need my wife. I need to feel the love I share with you, because I am about to bury my two younger brothers.” His voice lowered. “I am so fucking scared, Roni. So angry and so scared.”

Her hands moved to cover his cheeks, her thumbs wiped the tears that escaped his eyes. “I know, baby. Me too. But please don’t ask me to do this here. Take me to a hotel, or take me for a ride in the car. Anywhere but here. I don’t want to deny you the love we share, I would never do that to you. God, I love you so much, Joe. But please not here. Not in your mom’s house. Respect that I can’t.”

His mouth came down hard on hers. “I do, beautiful.” He moaned between kisses. “I do. I love you.”

They stood against the wall for some time just kissing and holding one another. The knock on the door pulled them from the dance. “Yeah?” Joe yelled.

“Mom wanted me to get you guys. Pastor Brad will be here soon.”

Joe reached over and opened the door. Roni ducked her head into his neck. Alex laughed at the position they were in. "Tell Mom we'll be down in a few minutes. Roni needs to wash her face."

Roni started to giggle, slapping Joe on the chest. Alex laughed and walked away.

"Oh my God. I'm so embarrassed. Put me down, Joe."

"I'm not done with you yet." He kissed her again, pressing his cock into her core. "After dinner, we are going for a drive."

Roni busted out laughing. As he set her down, she grabbed his cock. "You better get this under control. I'm sure Pastor Brad wouldn't understand." Turning, she walked out of the room and headed to the stairs.

"So not fair," Joe yelled after her, laughing.

Roni was giggling as she hit the bottom of the stairs. The doorbell rang. "Sally, you want me to get it?" she yelled as she reached for the door.

"Yes, thank you," Sally called as she walked through the living room.

Joe was coming down the stairs as she opened the door. There was a man standing with his back to the door dressed in black. Joe hit the floor as Sally came into the hall, and the man turned, looking right at Roni.

"What the fuck?" she whispered as she slammed the door shut. Turning, she tried to run away, but Joe grabbed her. "No!" she screamed. "No!" She fought with him, hitting him, and he finally let her go.

"Roni!" he yelled.

She turned as his mother opened the door. "Pastor Brad. I'm sorry, please come in."

Joe nearly had a stroke. The man at the door could have been Tony Eden's twin. "What the fuck?"

"Joseph, please, the language," his mother snapped.

The man went to step inside the house. "Oh, no you don't," Joe shouted. Grabbing the door out of his mother's hand, he shoved the man back and slammed the door, locking it. Turning to his mother, he said very quietly, "Get your ass in that safe room now." Turning to the stairs, he looked at Becca. "Take her and Alex now. Get in the safe room."

It was a commotion. Joe found Roni in the kitchen standing by the back door. Walking up behind her, he wrapped his arms around her waist. "Come on, sweetheart. I want you in the safe room." She nodded and let him lead her there. "I'll be back."

"Joseph, what is going on?" His mother was furious.

"Roni will explain. I'll be back. What is Pastor Brad's last name?"

"I'm not sure. Joseph, what in the world is going on?"

Joe looked at Roni. He could see she was shaking. "I'll be back," he said to her, shutting the door.

Al looked at him. "What the fuck is going on?"

"Come on, I'll show you." Joe led him back to the front door. When he opened it, the man was still standing there on the porch.

"What the fuck?" Al said.

"Gentlemen, is there a problem? Sally invited me over for dinner to discuss the burial of her sons. Who might you be?"

Joe chuckled as he moved his hand behind him, wrapping it around the butt of his gun. "Joe Blackshaw. Who are you?"

"Pastor Brad."

Al chuckled. "Yeah, we're going to need a bit more than that."

"Bradly Eden," the man said.

"Well, Bradly Eden, may I ask how old you are?" Al snapped at him.

"I don't understand what my age has to do with a dinner invitation, but I'm sixty-one."

"How long have you been in the clergy?" Joe asked.

The man stood there looking at them. "I'm sorry, I'm afraid I don't understand."

"Mr. Eden, we understand a great deal. I would appreciate it if you would answer the question. I can call the police, or better yet, I'll give my friends at the F.B.I. a call, then you can answer all their questions. Believe me when I tell you this, these questions are nothing compared to what will come from them." Al snarled at him.

"I've been in the clergy the majority of my adult life. What is this about?"

"You ever been married?" Joe asked.

"Yes. My wife died of cancer many years ago."

"Sorry for your loss. Do you have any children?" Al asked him.

Joe's grip on the gun tightened as he waited for an answer.

"I have three children. Two sons and a daughter." He smiled.

"Where are they?" Joe snapped at him.

"I'm not sure. I'm afraid that when my wife passed away, I took to the bottle. The children were taken from me when they were young." He put his head down as if he was ashamed of himself.

"Did you beat them, Mr. Eden?" Joe was trying very hard to contain his anger.

"I'm ashamed to admit it, but yes. I am not a good drunk."

Joe leaned into him. "I am going to say this to you just once. Your son, Tony, murdered my brothers. He nearly murdered me and my wife. You are going to turn around and walk away from this house, pack your bags, and move as far away from here as you can. If I find out you haven't, I am going to have the F.B.I. down your throat and then up your ass. Do you understand me, Mr. Eden? Don't ever come back here again."

The man stood there looking at Joe then Al. "I'm so sorry. I had no idea."

"Why would you? You see, Mr. Eden, you made your son an abusive piece of shit, a murderer, and you never looked back. You never went back to get your children, did you? You never went back to say you were sorry, did you?" The man shook his head.

Al stepped in front of Joe. "I'm going to check and make sure you have left town. If you can leave your children that fast and walk away from them when they need you, then I want you nowhere near my mother and my brother. I'm not going to threaten you, Mr. Eden. I'm stating the facts. If you don't leave this place, I will bury you next to your fucking low life piece of shit son. You understand me?"

The man stood there looking at Al. Joe watched him swallow hard. "Be careful, Mr. Eden. Be very careful."

He turned and walked down the driveway to his car. They watched as he drove down the street away from their mother's house. Joe turned and went to get Roni. Looking at his mother, he said calmly, "Al will explain everything to you. Roni and I will be back in the morning. We need to go."

Without saying a word, Joe took her hand, and they walked out of the house and got in the car. He drove them to a hotel and checked them in. When they got in the room, he wrapped himself around her. He knew she needed to cry, and he knew she was being brave for his mother. The minute her head hit his chest, the tears came. The sobs, the screams. He held on to her, kissing her head and crying with her. He couldn't help but wonder if the pain would ever stop for her. They still needed to see her father.

"God, baby, I am so sorry for that, for all of this. I love you," he whispered to her.

He felt her take a few deep breaths. Pulling away, she looked at him. "Who was he?"

Joe wiped her tears. "That was his father. He had no idea who Tony was as an adult. The children were taken away from him when they were younger. It's done, he's gone."

She nodded, looking around. With a small smile on her face, she asked, "Why are we here, Joe?"

"Because I know how brave you were being for my mom. I know how upset you are, and I wanted you to feel safe."

"Hmm," she mused, moving away from him and toward the bed. "Could it be that maybe you wanted to utilize the privacy this affords you?" She pushed on the bed with her hand.

Joe loved this about her, how she knew him so well. "That, at the time, was the furthest thing from my mind. But now that you bring it up..."

Roni giggled, pulling her shirt over her head. Joe didn't move as he licked his lips, his heart slamming in his chest. She was so beautiful. He watched as she unclipped her bra, freeing her extraordinary breasts. He felt his mouth water as her fingers undid her jeans.

Sliding them down her legs, she left her panties on for him. "Take your clothes off, husband. I want to watch," she whispered to him. Crossing his arms, he slowly pulled his t-shirt up his stomach, past his broad chest. "Wait, hold it there." Joe couldn't see her, but he felt her move closer to him. Nothing touched him except her mouth as she drew his nipple between her teeth, gently biting it then the other. He was going to release in his fucking jeans if she didn't stop. Stepping back, she whispered, "Continue, please."

His smile was huge as he pulled his shirt all the way off. "You want a show, sweetheart?"

"Mmm, yes please."

Her eyes were on fire with desire. God, he loved this woman. Slowly, he popped the top button on his jeans, watching as her tongue came out and licked her lips. The second button popped open on its own, he was so hard. When she saw his head, she smiled. "Stop." Her voice sent chills down his spine.

She stepped forward and bent down, licking his crown then taking the bit of cum off the tip. "Mmm, husband, you are my favorite flavor."

"Wife, if you don't stop, my jeans won't hit the floor before I explode." His voice was raspy with his need to come.

"I think I'd like to see that please." Her fingers popped the third button as she stepped back. "Don't touch yourself. Let me touch you. Let me make you cum."

Smiling, Joe popped the fourth button, and his jeans slid down his legs. Stepping out of them, he moved toward her. She was shaking her head. "Stop. Will you kneel on the edge of the bed, Joe, and close your eyes? Trust me."

He couldn't look away from her. The mischief in her eyes confused him. She was just hysterical. He wanted to hold her, maybe make love to her. "Can we talk for a minute?" His voice was soft and gentle.

Her eyes changed; she amazed him with the different expressions. "You don't want me to touch you?"

"With all that I am, but that's not what's important right now. I..." He was struggling to find the words without sounding like an asshole. "I can't do this. I can't just forget what happened, and I don't think you can either."

She shook her head. "I can't, but I want to. I want to, Joe. Let me. Let me forget because it doesn't matter to us anymore. Nothing should matter except burying your brothers, seeing my father, and telling him we love each other. Then we can live our life together. I just want to be happy. I want that with you."

He stepped forward, pulling her to him. "I want that, too, baby. But sweeping everything under the rug isn't going to make it go away. It will still be there when we walk out of this room in the morning. Making love isn't going to change what we have to face."

"You don't want to make love with me?"

"Oh, sweetheart, with everything that I am. But I want you there with me. I want you whole; I want us whole. That son of a bitch threw a wrench in my thinking today. If I was working this whole thing as a case, red flags would be up everywhere. They are up everywhere."

She pulled back. "Then why are we here? Why aren't we back there trying to figure it out?"

"I took us out of the situation so I could help you through this. I know how shaken up you were."

"Yes, but you can't do that. You have to allow me to fall apart. You have to allow me to be strong. I'm not some fragile little woman."

"Perhaps, but it's my job as your husband, as the man who loves you, to protect you."

Roni laughed. "You can't always save me, Joe. I won't ever grow as a person if you protect me all the time. When we have children and you are teaching them to ride a bike, are you going to pave the sidewalks with pillows so they don't get hurt when they fall down?"

Joe laughed. "Yes. But I understand what you are saying to me.

Come on, beautiful, let's get dressed and head back to my mom's. I want what you want. I want our life."

Her hand wrapped around his cock. "You sure?"

Joe closed his eyes and swallowed hard. "No, baby, I'm not. But it's the right thing to do. I want this with you, but I want us to be free of all this shit." She squeezed him as she slowly pumped him. "Mmm. You are not being fair." He groaned.

She wiped the pre-cum off his head with her thumb as she let go of him, bringing it to her mouth. Joe watched her slip her thumb between her lips and suck it off, smiling at him. "Have it your way."

He was a bit more forceful than he ever wanted to be with her when he grabbed her. "Oh, I am going to have it my way, and trust me, beautiful, you aren't going to be able to walk when I'm done."

"You don't scare me, Joe Blackshaw," she whispered on his lips as she crawled up his body, wrapping her legs around his hips. "You don't fucking scare me." Her mouth crashed down on his, her hands in his hair, her nails pushing into his scalp.

Joe was in heaven with her, with this woman who owned him. His hands pressed into her incredible plump ass. It was difficult not to rip her panties off and take her just like this.

"Do it, husband. Do it. Please, I need to feel you."

His feet were moving, pressing her against the wall. He shredded her panties. Her hips wiggled, and she managed to get his head inside her, and he let her go. She slid down him as he pushed up. He wanted to slam into her, but he knew it would hurt her. A few movements and they were going to town. He fucked her, and he fucked her hard. They bit each other, pulled each other's hair as they came undone.

Joe bent his knees, and they moved down the wall until Roni was sitting on his thighs. His hand was on her face. "What you make me feel…" he whispered to her. "I love you."

She smiled at him. "All of me, always, Joe. That's all I have to give you. All of me."

"It's all I want, baby."

They stayed like that for a long time, kissing and touching each other. It was the first time in his life that he felt so connected to another human being, so complete with who he was. She loved him no matter what lay ahead of them, it was just them. Together, they could do anything.

"Come on, beautiful. Let's go face this and move forward."

Roni nodded, kissing him again. "I love you. Thank you for this."

"I love you, and you never have to thank me for loving you."

CHAPTER THIRTEEN

When they walked back into his mother's house, she was up and moving toward Roni. "Oh, sweetheart, I am so sorry. I had no idea who he was. He has been nothing but kind to us, to his congregation. Can you ever forgive me?" She pulled Roni into her arms.

Roni had never had another woman hold her like this, care about her feelings like this. Her eyes moved to Joe's, whose were full of unshed tears. Roni hugged her, burying her face in Sally's neck, fighting her own tears. "Thank you, Sally."

The two women hugged for a few minutes, then Sally let go, grabbing Joe. "Thank you, Joey, for getting rid of him. I don't know what I would have done if I'd discovered this news after I let him do the service." She pulled back. "I think we should just have the funeral home do a nice little service at the gravesites."

"Sounds good to me. I'm sorry, Mom, I know how much you liked Pastor Brad."

"Perhaps, but I love my children more, and if one of them is in distress," she looked at Roni and smiled, "then I will do everything in my power to right the wrong." She stepped back. "Now, come on, we need to eat before we get going. Becca and Al need to get home, and you two need to get on with your honeymoon."

Roni looked at Joe, who was beaming at her. "Yes, our honeymoon." He smiled at her.

She giggled, and they all headed into the dining room to eat.

The service was short but nice. They buried Jason and Ben's ashes next to their sister. Standing there looking at her gave, he knew she was finally at peace. Kneeling, he put his hand on her headstone, whispering, "I love you." When he stood, Roni slipped her hand in his.

Together, they walked to the car. At his mother's house, everyone said goodbye. Al and Becca, along with Ella and Mr. Fluff, headed back to Idaho. Joe and Roni headed to D.C. to finally see her father.

Sitting in the car in the parking lot at Walter Reed Hospital, Roni looked at Joe. "I'm scared. I love my father, and I'm scared this is going to hurt him. That we are going to hurt him."

Joe swallowed. "He's been my friend for twenty years. I feel the same way. Why don't we take it minute by minute? I'll leave it up to you to tell him."

She smiled a small smile. "I love you."

"I love you. You ready?"

She nodded, and Joe got out of the car. Walking around, he opened her door for her, giving her his hand and helping her out. They walked hand in hand into the hospital. When they reached the hall that led to his room, Roni let go of his hand, her heart slamming in her chest the closer they got to his room. She had to stop herself from running.

The door was open, and she could hear him talking to someone, to her mother, which confused her. Why wasn't she in fucking jail? Turning, she looked at Joe, who seemed just as shocked as she was. Roni paused at the door to listen.

"Michael, I don't understand why you want a divorce," her mother said.

Roni smiled when she heard her father laugh. "Elizabeth, you haven't been faithful to me in twenty years. You are a horrible person, and I'm sure you had something to do with what Tony did to our daughter and to the Blackshaws."

"Why would you say that? How could you say that? Jason Blackshaw attacked Tony in our foyer. I had nothing to do with that."

"I think you need to leave. Sign the divorce papers, Elizabeth. I'll give you the house in L.A., but that's all you're getting from me."

Roni stepped into the room. "She shouldn't even get that. Her plan was to kill you then kill me and split the money with Tony. Wasn't it, Mother? Why are you here and not in jail?"

Roni looked at her father, whose face lit up like the fourth of July. "My God, Veronica. It's so good to see you. When Al called and told me what happened to you, I was beside myself."

Her mother stood, looking at her. "Well, Mother? Why aren't you in jail?"

Her mother's eyes shifted to the door where Joe stood. Roni smiled when she saw her swallow hard.

"The police are on their way, Mother. Apparently, you have been avoiding them. Well, not today."

Elizabeth didn't say a word. Her eyes locked on Joe's. Roni's father couldn't see Joe yet. He reached for her. "Come here, daughter, and give your old man a hug. I am so glad you are all right. When did you get your memory back?"

"A few days ago. I had a few things to do, but I'm here now, Daddy. How are you doing?"

"I'm good. I'll be released tomorrow. I'm so glad you are here. You can come and stay with me at the house."

"I would love that, but I can only stay for a day or two. Daddy, I need to tell you something." She looked at her mother who was still looking at Joe. "Well, both of you, actually." Her mother's eyes moved back to her. Roni smiled and looked at her father. "Daddy, this is going to be a shock to you, but I need for you to understand that we met long before either of us knew who the other was."

Her father smiled at her. "Veronica, what are you trying to say?"

Her smile lit up the room. "Daddy, I fell in love. I got married."

She saw her mother's head snap to the door. "Are you fucking kidding me?" she whispered.

"Elizabeth, what are you going on about?" her father asked.

"Daddy, please don't be upset."

Her mother was still looking at the door, looking at Joe, who was smiling. "You married my daughter?" He nodded.

"What?" Her father was trying to look around Roni. "He's here? I want to meet him."

"Daddy, he's waiting for the police, so mother can't get away this time. But you already know him." Her voice softened. "You've known him for twenty years."

Her father's head jerked toward her. His eyes filled with concern. "What are you saying, Veronica? Who did you marry?"

She swallowed. "I married Joe Blackshaw."

Her father didn't say a word. He just sat in the bed looking at her, his eyes shifting to the door then to her mother. It was the strangest thing, Roni thought, when he busted out laughing while he was looking at her mother. "Well, Elizabeth, you certainly aren't going to be able to sleep with him now." Her eyes moved to him. "I know you've tried for twenty years to fuck that man. It must really be the icing on the cake for you to know he loves our daughter and wants nothing to do with you."

"Honestly, Michael, I don't know what you mean. Joe Blackshaw means nothing to me." Her eyes shifted to Roni, filled with hatred.

Michael was still laughing when Roni smiled at her mother. "I was in the hallway listening to you try and come on to him. I'm sorry, Mother, but he was already mine then. He's been mine for a long time, and trust me when I tell you this. He is a hundred times the man Tony Eden was. So, yeah." Turning her head, she looked at her father. "Daddy, I'm sorry we didn't tell you. Joe has been beside himself, but if we had said anything, Tony would have found out. Neither of us wanted to hurt you."

Her father took her hand. "Am I upset? Yes and no. Joe is a bit older than you, but he is a good man. Yes, he is my friend, but I also know he wouldn't have married you if he didn't truly love you. Is this going to take some getting used to? Yes, it is. But looking at you and this smile on your face and the happiness in your eyes, I can see he is the best choice for you."

There were voices at the door. Roni turned to see the police walk in and arrest her mother for conspiracy to commit murder. "Goodbye, Mother. I just want you to know that, no matter what happens to you, I won't give you another thought."

Elizabeth hung her head as they put handcuffs on her.

Joe stood just outside the door. He was absolutely terrified at what Mike was going to say. But looking at Elizabeth, at the evil in her eyes and the lust as she glared at him, he actually felt a bit excited to see her face when Roni told Mike about them.

When he heard the words come out of her mouth, and Elizabeth snarled at him, he couldn't contain his smile. He wanted to scream "fuck you" at her, but she wasn't worth it.

"Excuse me. Did you call the police?" a voice asked.

Joe turned to see four policemen standing in the hall. "I did. I believe the Los Angeles police are looking for Elizabeth Holloway on conspiracy to commit murder charges."

"Yes, we have a warrant for her arrest. She is wanted by the Virginia and D.C. police as well for questioning about the attack on Senator Holloway. Do you know the whereabouts of Mrs. Holloway?"

"I do. She is right there." Joe moved so the officer could see her standing in the room.

"Thank you, Mister…?"

"Blackshaw, Joe Blackshaw."

"Well, thank you, Mr. Blackshaw."

Joe moved out of the way as the men walked into the room. He stood there smiling while they cuffed her. As she walked past Joe, she stopped, "I would have never pegged you to want a spoiled, fat-assed princess."

Joe busted out laughing. Leaning in, he whispered. "You don't have a clue the woman your daughter is. She is a hundred times more than you will ever be."

"Fuck you, Joe Blackshaw," she snarled.

"No thank you, Elizabeth."

He watched as they hauled her off. Hopefully, he would never have to deal with that woman again. When he heard Mike say his name, his heart stopped. If he was being honest, he would say he was more than nervous. When he stepped into the room to face his friend, he was greeted with a smile.

When he walked over to the bed, Mike put his hand out to shake his. "I'll say this," Mike began. "I'm a bit more than surprised."

Joe shook his hand. "You aren't the only one."

"Joe, we've known each other for a long time, so this is going to take a bit to get used to, but I will say that I know you are not the kind of man who would do something like this lightly. I know Veronica is in good hands."

Joe looked up to see Roni beaming. His smile was automatic. "Mike, we didn't know each other. I didn't know who she was until I brought her home that night. We tried to stay away from each other, but she had me the second I met her."

Mike was smiling at the love he saw in their eyes. "She couldn't have picked a better man. Like I said, it's going to take some time, but I can see she is happy, and that's all I can ask for. She is my only daughter, and with you being an old man," Mike chuckled, "is it too much to still hope for some grandchildren?"

Joe busted out laughing. "You're older than me. But to answer your question, I can only hope."

Roni smiled at him. "Oh, there will be. One day. We've got some living to do first." She turned to look at her father. "Thank you, Daddy, for not wanting to kill him. I know he is your friend, and we both struggled with this, especially Joe, once he found out I was your daughter. But I convinced him that this wasn't about the two of you, but us."

"You're right. I know he's a good man, the best, and as difficult as it is for me to grasp, I'm not arrogant enough to think you don't deserve to be happy, either of you."

"Thanks, Mike."

~

Roni couldn't have been happier with her father's reaction. They stayed at the hospital for most of the day. "We'll be back to get you tomorrow and take you home," she told her father as she hugged him.

"Where are you staying? Why don't you stay at the house? I'm sure they cleaned up the mess."

"I don't think I can, Daddy. It's hard enough knowing what he did to everyone. We will be fine, and we'll be here first thing to get you."

"I understand, darling. I'll see you in the morning." He kissed her on the cheek, shook Joe's hand, and then they left.

Walking out into the night, Joe pulled her against his side. "Let's get something to eat and find a place to sleep."

"Oh, Mr. Blackshaw, eating and sleeping is not what I want or need right now," she whispered against his chest.

"Jesus, Roni." He chuckled.

She had a renewed bounce in her step. Her heart was finally full. Finally happy.

~

As they walked through the parking lot, Joe felt his life come full circle. The ring in his pocket from his mother would rest on her finger for the rest of his life. He found it; he found her. It may not have started out like it should have, and the road to where they were now was hard-won and untraditional, but the completeness he felt throughout his heart, mind, body, and soul was the end result he could have only ever dreamed of.

www.ingramcontent.com/pod-product-compliance
Lightning Source LLC
LaVergne TN
LVHW091146080826
845145LV00008B/2280

9780998974866